By the same author

Buckmaster
Buckmaster and the Cattlelifters
Mojave Wipeout
Buscadero
Miserywhip's Last Stand
A Devil Called Clegg
Santosbrazzi Killer
Tumbleweed
Devil's Spawn
The Undertaker
Fyngal's Gold
Night Stalker
Bareknuckle Fighter
The Chiseller
The Coffin Filler
The Grandstanders
Breakout
Mustang Round-Up
The Dam-Breakers
Retribution Trail
Tenderfoot on the Trail

The Horse Wrangler

Gus Strang, a veteran of the Civil War who spied and killed for General Robert E. Lee, has become a cold-hearted assassin. But he is not prepared for his dying mother's confession that the man he had always thought to be his father, was not his father. His real father had thrown his mother off his ranch when she became pregnant.

After his mother's death, Strang leaves Texa to seek out his father in Montana, hell-bent o revenge. He little realizes just what complicatio will arise, or how his life will change forever.

The Horse Wrangler

TEX LARRIGAN

Western

ONDON

ISBN 0 7090 7338 0

Robert Hale Limited
Clerkenwell House
Clerkenwell Green
London EC1R 0HT

Typeset by
Derek Doyle & Associates, Liverpool.
Printed and bound in Great Britain by
Antony Rowe Limited, Wiltshire

ONE

The stranger drew rein and watched the galloping herd of horses, pounding hoofs sounding like distant thunder. He wondered what had disturbed them from the feeding-grounds down in the valley.

He reached for his old army field glasses while patting his mare's neck, for she was growing restive and the horse-smell on the wind was reminding her of her early days of freedom.

'Steady on, old girl.' His easy tone made her flick her ears. She whinnied in reply and tossed her head.

He followed the fast moving herd with the glasses. He saw at once that the lead stallion was flanked by the younger stallions, protecting the mares and foals in a tight inner group. They were well trained, no doubt by an old experienced stallion. But why the organized exodus from such a lush valley?

Then the roving glasses caught the faint puffs of smoke. He frowned and swore under his breath. Someone was down there who had deliberately caused the stampede. But why?

He decided to investigate. He gave the mare a gentle kick in the ribs and she moved forward in a gentle canter that soon turned into a fast loping gallop. This was what the black mare loved, to let her muscles stretch in a rippling even gait which she could keep up for hours.

Gus Strang felt again the union between man and horse. Susie, named after a girl back East, was his best friend. He could trust her far more than he could trust any man . . . or woman.

Now they were heading for the herd; soon they would pass him by. Already he was breathing in their dust. He pulled his bandanna over his nose and mouth. There was also a strong smell of sweat and of fear. Gus knew the smell of horse-fear well. He'd encountered it many times, during the war and the early years afterwards.

But those days were done. Wild herds had been rounded up. He'd done his share of rounding up on behalf of the army. They had had to replenish the stocks of army horses depleted by war.

This herd of mustangs must belong to someone

and it looked very much as if someone down below in the valley was on a rustling caper.

He drew rein when he saw the leading stallion pass by, close enough to see his tossing head and flaring nostrils. The herd pounded after him. It would take some while before the punishing speed would slacken.

Gus turned Susie so that they rode at one side of the herd, shrouded in dust. With luck they might come upon the men responsible for the stampede.

Gus Strang had a personal interest in that herd. If his suspicions were correct, they belonged to a man he'd travelled a thousand miles to confront.

He thought of his mother's dying words and his mouth set in a hard line.

Yes, for her sake he had to face Jed Wildsmith.

He wondered what he would be like. He would be an old man now, pushing seventy. Would he remember Rosita Gonzales, the seventeen-year-old girl he'd seduced forty years ago?

He remembered the shock when Rosita told him that Ned Strang was not his father. He'd worshipped Ned as a young boy. Ned had taught him to shoot and fish and they'd gone camping together and Ned had taught him to read sign and made a game of it, so that in time, the young Gus had become a survival expert, knowing where to dig for edible roots, where the bees would likely conceal their hives, and how to follow the spoor of small animals.

Ned had been a blacksmith and, what was most important, he'd loved horses and taught Gus everything he now knew. Ned had shaped his life as it was today.

Not once had Ned betrayed by look or deed that he was anything other than a devoted father. They'd shared so many good memories and even though Ned had passed away more than twelve years ago, Gus still missed his cheery grin and hearty laughter.

So his mother's dying words had come as a devastating shock. It hadn't made any difference for Gus's love and respect for the man he called father, but there had been a growing anger in him that there was a man somewhere in Montana who'd used his mother so ruthlessly.

It had taken him three months to reach Montana and the Powder River from his home in Texas. Each night, as he'd bedded down, he'd renewed his vow to his dead mother that he would seek Jed Wildsmith out and take revenge.

He was vague as to what he should do when he finally caught up with Wildsmith. It would all depend on how Wildsmith reacted when he gave it to him straight. *I'm your son. You remember Rosita Gonzales? The young girl from the wagon train whom you took in as a housekeeper and seduced, and whom you threw out when she told you she was pregnant?*

He often wondered what the man's reaction to those words would be.

But now all personal thoughts left him as he and Susie raced down into the valley floor, intent on surprising whoever was out there. The dust being raised obscured his approach.Whoever was out there couldn't see him and he couldn't see them. So, when he finally found himself at the tail-end of the herd and the dust had cleared somewhat, he was surprised to find he'd come slap bang into the back of a crouching figure hiding behind a boulder, who was intent on loading up a businesslike repeating rifle and returning fire that was coming from more than a hundred yards away.

Whoever was crouching low was so intent on his target that he didn't hear Gus's approach.

A stray bullet whined past Gus's head, which made him dismount mighty sharpish and slap Susie on her rump so that she trotted out of range. Then cocking his Peacemaker, he sprang across the rough ground, dodging behind the rearing boulder.

The crouching figure swivelled round at the click of the gun, half-rose and then thought better of it as the bullets chipped the surrounding rock.

'You'd better get your head down,' a woman's voice drawled, 'unless you want to get it blown off!' Gus dropped down beside her.

'What's going on here?'

The woman risked a quick glance at him before turning to fire again at the clump of trees.

'You a stranger to these parts? You must be or else you'd know that there's a horse war going on. Those bastards out there are rustlers. At least I reckon Jed Wildsmith and his men are rustlers!'

Gus raised an eyebrow. 'You know Jed Wildsmith?'

The girl laughed bitterly. 'I should do. I grew up alongside him with my pa and ma. I'm still hanging on to our homestead even though Wildsmith's tried to get me out.'

'Why should he do that?'

'Because he wants the whole range. He's bought out other homesteaders, either by bribing them with cash or threatening them. I'll not be bribed or threatened.'

'And those horses?'

'They're *my* horses. Me and my men rounded up those wild mustangs and one of Wildsmith's bastards let them out of their corral. They

wounded one of my men. He's out there somewhere still alive unless the horses stampeded
over him. Poor Billy.' Her voice wavered before she
took another shot.

They both heard a scream and the girl smiled
grimly at Gus.

'That's for Billy!'

'Where's the rest of your men?'

'The rest?' Again she laughed, but bitterly.

'If you can describe old Carlos and his grand-
son, Jacko, and Lew, who's as lame as the rest,
they'll be hiding out somewhere until the ruckus
dies down. Everyone's scared of the Wildsmith
outfit.'

'Mmm, so we'll have to do something about this
stand-off. How many men have you got holed up
there, d'you think?'

'Four, and at least one of them's hurt.'

'So I take it they can't move from that stand of
trees?'

'No. The trees are on the rim of a gorge into the
next valley. As you see, there's no cover. It's just a
matter of time.' She grinned.

'So, let's lure them out. I'm an impatient man. I
like to get things done.'

'How do we do that?'

'Next time they give you a broadside, scream as
if you're hit. Then we wait.'

'And then?'

'When you don't fire back they'll think it safe to come out. They'll be keen to get after those horses.'

'Then we pick them off?'

'You got it, lady. We pick them off!'

So they waited and Gus helped things along by sending a couple of shots into the undergrowth at about the height of a man's chest, which brought an immediate response.

'Right! Now a good scream!' The girl obliged with a yell that would have done an Indian proud.

They waited. Then came movement in the bushes under the trees. First one man and then another cautiously stepped forth. A third man, holding another upright, staggered out. They all looked around. Everything was still.

Gus and the girl watched as one man, who seemed to be in charge, gave an order and a young boy started to run towards them.

'Huh,' Gus said softly, ' he's coming to find out whether you're dead or not. Now when I say fire, let 'em have it, and don't hesitate. It's either them or us, remember.'

The girl, looking white, nodded. It was one thing firing into bushes and trees but another actually aiming to kill a man.

Gus waited, counting to five in his mind. Then

he said sharply, as if back commanding his troops in the army:

'*Fire!*' His Colt took the man in charge in the throat and his second shot blasted the second man as his gun came up to return fire. All the while Gus was aware of the girl blasting away beside him.

It was all over in a matter of minutes and only the smell of burnt gunpowder remained amid a haze of smoke.

The girl turned and smiled at him. She was a plain wench, he thought, and older than he'd first judged. Her face was tanned and the sun had carved wrinkles around the eyes. But they were warm, brown eyes and her wide mouth had a certain charm.

'Thank God you came along!' She held out a work-worn hand. 'I'm Kate Marshall and I belong over at the Double M ranch.

She spoke as if Gus should know the Double M.

'Gus Strang,' he said briefly and her grip was that of a man. Then he nodded to the bodies.

'Anyone you know?'

'Nope! Jed Wildsmith's brought in some professional gunmen since he decided to take over the range. Me and some of the other homesteaders make sure we don't meet up with them.'

'So what do we do now?'

'We? There's no call for you to become involved in our troubles, Mr Strang.'

'Call me Gus. Everyone else does.'

'Then you must call me Kate.'

'Very well, Kate. What do we do now?'

'I'm going to round up those of the neighbours who are sitting tight and go after that herd. There's more than just mine in that bunch. There'll be some sorting out to be done.'

'What if they're running with Wildsmith's own herd?'

'No. Jed Wildsmith's too wily to let that happen. He wants no trouble with the law. We can't finger him as a rustler. What he wants is to disrupt our lives. Make difficulties for us. Those horses will be driven a couple of days' ride from here and the stallions will separate their own groups from each other for fear the mares will take off after other stallions.'

Gus nodded. He knew too well that stallions didn't tolerate other stallions living close by on their territory. He was in a dilemma. Should he go ahead and help this girl, or make for the Wildsmith ranch as he'd intended?

Kate's slumped shoulders and bowed head decided him. What the hell . . . he'd waited so long to confront Jed Wildsmith, he could wait a bit longer.

'If you tell me what you want me to do, I'll get on with it.'

Kate looked at him in doubtful surprise.

'You mean it. You'd really help us? You don't know me. I could be spinning you a yarn.'

'I don't think so. Besides, I can quit any time I like, so stop jawing and let's have some action!'

They located their horses and mounted up. Secretly, Kate admired the black mare with the shiny coat. It showed Gus Strang was a caring man. She also liked the way he didn't dig his spurless heels into the horse's ribs when they broke into a gallop. He knew how to get the best out of his mount with the least effort.

They did not speak as they rode along. Gus's eyes continually wandered over the terrain and found it good. No wonder Jed Wildsmith coveted this range. Good feed, good protection and water far below. Yes, all good God-given land and ideal for breeding cattle and horses.

They came at last to a long wire fence, now broken down, posts sagging and the barbed wire a hazard for any animal. They drew up and surveyed the damage. Gus's mouth tightened.

'They did that? Your land?'

'Yes.'

'How come you were herding them all together?'

'The army agents had been making the rounds. They're still buying in mustangs. Me and some of the other small ranchers thought it a good thing to round up what we had to sell and let the agent arrange for their dispatch. The only way we could control the youngsters was by bringing in the herds to keep 'em quiet. So, as I had the biggest corral, the horses were brought to me. There were forty-three animals, counting the foals, in that corral last night. Now I've to tell three neighbours that their herds have been stampeded off our range. They're going to be mighty cross!'

'How many men can they muster?'

Kate shrugged. 'None of us can afford to pay wages, mister. I guess Donny Oakes is the best off. He has three grown sons. The other two make do with a couple of old men and a few boys.'

'Not exactly an army to fight professionals with!'

Kate sighed. 'We didn't expect this. Wildsmith's been busy stocking up his new land. Sheriff Woodley from our local township gives all us small ranchers any news that's going the rounds. We thought maybe he was satisfied with what he'd got. Now it looks as if he's starting all over again.'

'Can't the sheriff do anything?'

'No. He says he's got to have proof. Wildsmith's

men don't actually rustle the cattle and horses, just stampede them and cause us mayhem.'

'So while you're hunting stock, you can't do any other chores. That's it, isn't it? Harassment.'

'Yes, ' she answered simply. 'For a small outfit like mine, it can be disastrous. Young stock not looked after properly, fields not tilled. All us small ranchers try to be self-sufficient.'

Gus nodded thoughtfully while they picked their way through wire and then rode at a gentle pace the rest of the way to Kate's homestead.

Gus's eyes roved over it and the surrounding country as they approached the ranch house and the group of buildings around it. All were built of rough logs, a sure sign that in the very beginning cash had been tight. But whoever had decided to build on that spot had an eye for beauty, for the view was breathtaking.

A shallow, slow-moving stream, which presumably tumbled into the larger Powder River further down the valley, passed close by, making the watering of stock easy. A flat verdant pasture lay ahead and behind it a series of wooded slopes. To the right of the ranch, land had been ploughed and was a checkerwork of vegetable plots surrounded by a makeshift fence of barbed wire to guard against hungry cattle and horses.

It was a spot he himself would have chosen for such a ranch. He smiled at Kate.

'You've got a spread worth fighting for!'

She nodded. 'My father thought so. He spent his life building this place up. He even defended it against Indians. But of course he had more help than I have.'

'What happened to him?' The question was asked bluntly.

Her face clouded.

'Shot through the heart. He'd a good reputation as a breeder of good horses and some son of a bitch coveted his stallion. The man got away but the stallion didn't.'

'How come?'

'I shot him!'

Gus raised his eyebrows. '*You shot him?*'

'Yes. I was very young. I should have aimed for the man but I hadn't the guts. So I reckoned I'd rather kill the horse than have him used by that bastard.'

'You know who the man was?'

'No. He had his face covered but I have my suspicions.'

'So?'

She shrugged her shoulders and dismounted.

'It happened fifteen years ago. I'll never know for certain now. But one thing's for sure, they'll have to carry me off this place in a box!'

Gus slowly dismounted and tied up Susie to the hitching rail in front of the ranch. There was a wide veranda and Gus noted the two rocking-chairs placed there. The view faced south so that it would be pleasant to sit there after a day's hard work. Yes, the lady had a good set-up. He wondered whether there was a special man in her life.

They went inside to a long low room, cool and airy. Deer-antlers adorned the rough walls. There had been no attempt to plaster and decorate. All was functional: plain wood floor with only a buffalo-hide in front of a fat-bellied stove, rough handmade furniture and shelves that held an assortment of articles like books and boxes of ammunition, a pretty tin box, a bag of nails and what he presumed was a loaded revolver. Not the kind of place he associated with a woman.

She watched him look around as she flung her hat down on a brassbound chest. She smiled ruefully.

'Not the kind of place you expected? It's just as Father left it. I haven't changed a thing. What was good enough for him is good enough for me.' She busied herself putting the coffee-pot on to the stove and throwing a log into the fire. There was a sudden roar as the draught reddened the embers and the log burned.

'And what about your mother?'

'She never knew this place. I was three when she died on the trail. Father said it was smallpox that killed her. He said it was a miracle that I lived.'

'Mmm, evidently you didn't get it from her.' He was surprised to see her blush a little.

'No. When the smallpox first broke out in the caravan, all the children were put in charge of a couple who had no children of their own and they travelled alongside the caravan. No one was allowed to visit them. The older children, I'm told, used to wave to their parents to let them know they were fit and well. I of course was too young to remember much about it.'

'So he made a home for you both here, single-handed?'

'Yes, he often told me of the first terribly hard years before old Joe came along with his wife and son and settled here. That's why I'll never allow anyone to take this place from me!'

There was the smell of coffee on the air. Kate poured for them both, then brought out of a cupboard a loaf of bread and a leg of pork. She cut generous slices of meat and gave Gus a thick sandwich in his hand.

'There, that'll stop your guts grumbling.' She grinned and made herself a sandwich.

'Where are your men now?' Gus asked with his mouth full.

'I expect they're in the barn with Stormy and Betsy,' she said casually as she ate.

'Stormy and Betsy?'

'Yes. Stormy's my best stallion. Thank God, Betsy was nearly ready to mate. She can be a windy bitch if she's not spot on and once bit Stormy as he tried to mount her. That was when she had her last foal. Incidentally, the foal's in that stampeding herd. I hope to God he's not lamed. I was reckoning on getting a good price for him as a yearling.'

Again Gus nodded. He knew better than most how crucial it was to get stallion and mare together just at the right time. It could all go so terribly wrong.

'Would you like me to take a look? I know quite a bit about horse-breeding.'

'You?' Kate looked surprised. 'You're quite a useful fellow to know, aren't you? Actually you would be doing me a favour. Joe's getting old and Billy is inexperienced and we've been having trouble. Stormy gets too keen and becomes frustrated and lashes out.'

'Come on, let's get the priorities right. The herd can wait. If you've got a good stallion and there's a mare to be covered, then let's get at it!'

Kate led the way across the yard to the largest building apart from the ranch house itself. They could hear the sound of hoofs pounding the inner wall. Kate swore.

'That's Stormy. Betsy must be playing him up.' She opened one of the double doors and they both stepped inside. The barn was lit by one small window and the yellow light from a hurricane-lamp.

Gus saw an old man and a boy trying to hold the mare in a harness while the most beautiful stallion he had ever seen fought the bucking mare to mount her.

Both horses were covered in foam and sweat and in Gus's eyes there was a good chance that the stallion would do untold damage to the mare if he came down too hard on her.

'Here, let me take over,' he said to the surprised old man. 'You back Stormy away from her and let me quieten the mare. Walk the stallion round and round, and you, boy, bring me a brush and comb.'

'But the mare's just about ready—'

'Just do as I say!'

Kate watched as Gus gently patted the trembling mare, running his hands over her head and nose so that she could breathe in his scent. Then he slowly ran his hand over her back and sides and down her front legs. When the boy brought the brush and curry-comb, she stood quietly with her head hanging low but her ears twitched a little in response to Gus's rhythmic strokes.

Kate wondered just who Gus was and where he'd come from. What she did know was that Gus had a magical touch with horses. It was an inborn gift and she wished that he could stay with her for ever.

the blood and urine, goin' to spend an awful lot on it...

...sitte to respond to DDS' medication method.

Kate smothers out the Camaro and where it comes from. Where the pain ama was of the rough road...

...will tell that he could stay with us for ever.

TWO

Old Joe looked at the damaged fence in disgust, scratching his bald head and spitting.

'That there fence is gonna take a lot of time to put right, Kate. I ain't as slick as I used to be. No sir! That pesky varmint wants shooting! One of these days someone's going to do him in. Mark my words!' he finished darkly.

'Just as long as it's not you or me blamed for doing it, someone would be doing us a favour,' Kate answered lightly, but her brooding gaze was on Gus. She wondered . . . and then she drew herself up sharply. Hell! It had come to a pretty pass when she was considering a man's murder!

She turned abruptly away from the two men. Gus was already inspecting posts and post-holes.

'I wonder how long it will take Jacko to round

up the neighbours,' she asked to change the subject. Joe spat again.

'It'll depend. Jock McGovern is a crotchety man. He'll lay the responsibility on us. He'll reckon that as his horses were in our charge we should get 'em back. He's mean, is Jock.'

'But Charlie and his boys and Kit Fowler will be over pronto. I reckon it's time to get us some supplies rustled up and be ready to ride.'

'Hey now, you don't expect me to ride with you? Someone's got to stay behind and start on that fence or you've no corral to come back to.' Joe looked meaningfully at Gus. 'Besides, you got yourself another man to help you!'

Kate bit her lip. Joe was making it embarrassingly plain that he thought she had caught a man at last. She'd have a quiet word with him in private when she had time.

But suddenly she was conscious of work-stained shirt and muddy pants and she knew she must smell because she was usually too tired after a day's work to carry water, heat it and pour it into the old tin bath. Then again, how could she know she might meet a stranger, especially one who would have the guts to horn in on a fight that wasn't his.

At least he'd seen her at her worst and didn't seem shocked by what he saw. That was a comfort.

She glared at Joe who chuckled and turned away.

'Let's get back to Annie and see what she's got for us.'

'Annie?'

A cloud passed over Kate's face.

'She was Billy's mother, you know, the boy we buried.' She bit her lip. 'She's my housekeeper. I need one,' she added defensively, 'as I work alongside the men. That's why we're so rough and ready.' She felt herself apologizing and was angry.

Gus nodded. 'My ma worked alongside my pa; while he blacksmithed, she did the chores around the place. She could birth a calf or a foal as easy as birthing a baby. She was mighty cool. Nothing fazed her.' He spoke so casually, it was as if it was the usual thing for women to work alongside their menfolk.

Kate suddenly felt at ease.

Annie was a comfortably fat woman with a usually cheerful face. Now, her mouth was drawn down at the corners, her eyes showing her grief. She was compulsively kneading bread-dough.

'Sit you down and I'll pour you coffee. I was expecting you, Kate. I've put up some grub for you. You'll be off after the horses.' She looked at Kate. 'I expect they'll be heading in the same direction as last time?'

Gus also glanced at Kate. Last time? The woman sounded so matter of fact, as if it was an everyday occurrence.

'Yes, I guess so.' Kate sighed. 'Unless of course, Wildsmith has something else in mind.'

Annie stared at her.

'What could he have in mind?'

'You know he gave us a warning last time. It said get out or pay the consequences.'

'That was a lot of hot air to frighten you! He's a cunning old fox. He don't want any actual proof that he's mixed up with these here raids. After all, no horses are taken. They're all accounted for. It's just the botheration of getting 'em back!'

'But this time it's different These horses were all hand-picked by army vets, approved and ready for transport to army quarters. We don't get paid until they're delivered.'

'Well, that's no sweat. You'll get them back and the deal will go on.' Annie went on punching dough.

'Only if they're in good condition!'

Annie stopped what she was doing and looked at Kate in horror.

'You don't mean that they would actually chase them up into Devil's Canyon?'

Kate nodded. 'I mean just that.' She turned to

Gus. 'Devil's Canyon is a long narrow gulch and the entrance is a turn-off in the next valley. It winds its way along the next mountain range. Not a place to be marooned in. It's narrow and deep and gets little real daylight. There's no ground fodder and the way is littered with rocks and boulders. I reckon that thousands of years ago it was a river and what we see is the dry bed. A herd of horses turned galloping into that canyon could mean broken legs and a pile-up of bodies!'

Gus jumped to his feet.

'I get the picture. So you think Jed Wildsmith would go as far as that?'

She nodded.

'Then what are we waiting for? Let's get riding!'

'But what about the neighbours?'

'They'll get the picture. They'll follow on.'

It was easy to follow the trail of the herd. They made good time and Gus marvelled in the resilience of the woman. It was like riding with another man.

He took time to look about him as they rode. A good country to settle in. He could understand a man wanting to own it all. What he couldn't understand was the mentality of a man who could ride roughshod over his neighbours.

They stopped to eat and then pushed on. Now

Kate was moody. She had told Gus about the latest threat. The old man was becoming increasingly vicious.

'How many times has your stock been stampeded?'

'Six . . . seven times in four years. The last time resulted in the Farrers and the Hoskins selling out. This time . . .' she shrugged her shoulders. 'Tom Kingsly and Luke Stratton need some ready cash fast. I don't know about Jesse Lowe, but I know the chance to sell to the army was a godsend to us all.'

They were bedding down for the night when the sound of horses' hoofs alerted them and a bunch of horsemen rode into the clearing. Gus's reaction was to reach for his guns. But as a stentorian voice shouted, 'Kate! it's me and the boys!' Kate sat up, flinging her blanket from her.

'It's all right, Gus. It's Tom and the others.' She sprang up and ran across to the big man getting stiffly out of his saddle.

'Tom! Am I glad to see you!'

Gus watched as she flung her arms about big, greying Tom and hugged him.

'We came as soon as we got ourselves organized. That pesky son of a bitch wants lynching! I'm getting too old to be out chasing runaway horses! Any coffee on the go?'

The men crowded around the nearly dead fire but a poke amongst the embers and a few dry branches soon had a good fire going again and the coffee-pot, which was half-full, soon started to bubble.

Gus counted the men: more than he'd expected. A total count of eight and all looking as if they could handle themselves well. Kate was introducing him to the three neighbours who looked him over curiously.

'Howdy,' he said to them all. 'Pleased to meet you.'

'So how come you're in these parts,' asked old Tom bluntly.

Gus fixed him with a steely eye and Tom backed off. This feller wasn't going to take no shit. He rubbed a bristly chin.

'Look, I'm here to help Miss Kate. You don't need testimonials for me to do that. What and who I am is no business of anybody's. Right?'

Tom nodded, hunkered down by the fire and gulped at his coffee. Let Kate deal with him.

It was Jesse Lowe who asked the question they all wanted to be answered.

'Well? Who's taking charge of this here outfit?'

The men all looked at Kate, who looked worried.

'Jacko will have told you about the killings?'

'Yes,' Tom said heavily. 'It's going to make a mighty lot of difference. It's not just a matter of a stampede but of murder. Jed Wildsmith's not going to take it lying down.'

'That's why we need someone who's had experience to lead us.' Kate faltered. 'A professional. I think we've got such a man with us.' She looked at Gus.

'Gus. . . ?'

Gus was startled. Did it show so much that he was what one might describe as a professional killer? What made him so different from other men?

He coughed to give himself time to think. It was one thing helping out but another to assume command. There would be resentment from Kate's neighbours. It was only human nature. He was a stranger and as far as they were concerned, not to be trusted.

'Look, fellers, I'm not here to lead. I'll advise but let Tom here be the boss. I reckon we should start at the crack of dawn and get after those horses, turn 'em back and let those two young fellers herd 'em home and the rest of us make for this here Jed Wildsmith's ranch and teach him a little lesson.' He looked around at the listening men. 'Now that's my advice. Take it or leave it.'

The men looked at each other. Kate looked

worried. Jesse Lowe said cautiously;

'We've never given Wildsmith a visit before. We're not wanting to start a range war. That way we could be all dead.'

Gus shrugged, lit a cigarette and drew smoke into his lungs.

'It's your decision. It's not my business. As I said, I could ride away any time.'

He continued to smoke, watching them all with narrowed eyes. He'd lied when he said it wasn't his business. It was the best way he could think of to meet up with Jed Wildsmith. After all, why had he come to these parts but to seek out Wildsmith for revenge?

He saw Kate's apprehension, old Tom's cautious mistrust and the confusion amongst the rest of the men. Jesse Lowe had said it all for them. They didn't want a range war.

Tom Kingsly looked at the other men.

'What you say, guys? Do we take this here stranger's advice or not?'

'I say we should go find the herd. That's our first priority,' Luke Stratton chipped in. He was a slow, even-tempered man, who thought a lot and said little but when he spoke folk listened.

There were nods of agreement and Luke Stratton's son, Les, spat on the ground.

'I say Pa's right. Let's hit the hay and stop

jawing and get after them there horses! We need 'em badly. Our next winter's supplies depend on the cash our horses make.'

There was a general agreement. The men were walking away to unload bedrolls when Gus said, clear and bitingly:

'So you let that bastard get away with it again? No wonder he plays games with you! You ask for all the trouble you get!'

Jesse Lowe swung around on him.

'Now see here, mister, we don't need no shit from you!' He raised his fist as Gus sprang to his feet in one swift movement. Jesse found himself looking into the barrel of a firmly held Peacemaker. His eyes widened, as his fist stayed in mid-air while he raised his other hand.

'OK! OK! No need for violence, mister! I'm only objecting to your slur. We can fight if we have to but none of us wants that, do we, fellers? We just want to live peaceful lives and make a living. There's enough room on this range for all. It's that snake in the grass, Wildsmith, who's so greedy he wants the lot!'

Gus put his gun back in his holster. They noted his slick movements and that the holster was greased for a quick draw.

Kate intervened, trying to defuse the situation. 'Look, let's all get a good night's sleep and be ready to ride at dawn. We'll locate the horses and head them home and then see what happens. Remember, there's men dead back there. Wildsmith's not going to take that lightly. We might be forced to fight!'

The men went off, talking to each other. Gus lay down and watched the fire flicker in the darkness. Whatever those men decided to do, he was going to confront Jed Wildsmith. He lay awake a long time, wondering about the man. He had the hollow feeling that he took after his real father. Both of them were professional killers.

The trail of pounding hoofs was easy to follow. It cut through a pass in the mountain range and along another valley, well-watered and lush of grass. But there were signs that the herd had been frightened again and, as Kate had predicted, when they came to the junction that led to the Devil's Canyon there were signs that a brushwood fence had been erected and that the herd had swung left and charged into the dark narrow canyon.

Kate's heart sank. This was what she had dreaded. They could now be following a trail of dead or dying animals.

Tom Kingsly called a halt.

'It's no good going hell for leather up that there

gorge! We've got to make a plan. I think it's time we ate and thought this over. It could be a long time to our next meal.'

'Yes, you're right,' Luke Stratton agreed. The quiet man looked worried. 'I've never been in the Devil's Canyon myself, but they say it's an eerie place. No water and very little grass, and not much daylight. I've heard tell there are ghosts.'

'Stow it! There's no such thing as ghosts,' Gus said sharply as some of the listening men looked uneasy. 'Probably some made-up yarn to keep folk away! Could be a robber's hideout up there,' he finished half jokingly to ease the tension.

Jesse Lowe shook his head.

'That canyon's been taboo ever since earliest Indian times. I heard tales when I was a kid. My pa once nearly got himself killed when he was a boy because he went up that cursed gorge during some Indian ritual. He said they were dancing round a fire which was built around a huge needle of rock and they were howling like coyotes.'

Gus looked interested.

'Then what happened?'

'Some Indian kid who was a look-out, spied my pa crouched down watching and he let out a yell, but the dancers never heard him. They were making such a racket. Pa jumped the boy and knocked him down and the lad stared up at him thinking Pa would kill him, but Pa hadn't the guts to do that, so he knocked him out and scarpered.'

'He was lucky,' Gus murmured. 'Any white man spying on secret Indian rituals would not only be sacrificed but his whole family could be slaughtered too.'

Jesse Lowe spat on the ground.

'That wasn't the end of the matter. Years later, Pa was in a skirmish with the Indians. He was shooting and hiding behind a boulder when an Indian came down on him from behind. They fought and Pa had no chance. The Indian was too much for him and it was only when he was on his back looking up at his foe who had a knife ready to cut his throat, that they recognized each other. The Indian laughed, showing his teeth and said softly, "now I pay my debt and am under no obligation," and he knocked my pa out. When he woke up he was alone and had a sore jaw for weeks afterwards!'

'A great tale,' Gus said, 'but that was years ago. Does anyone know if Indians still live in this Devil's Canyon?'

They all shook their heads.

'We steer clear of this place,' Tom Kingsly confessed. 'We'll have to go up there cautiously and get behind those horses and drive 'em out as fast as we're able.' He looked at Kate. 'I think we should leave Miss Kate behind to look after this here camp. It might not be very pleasant up there.'

'No way,' Kate said firmly. 'My stock as well as yours is up there and I've got a strong stomach. I'm coming with you!'

Tom Kingsly shrugged.

'Have it your way, Miss Kate. An extra hand is always useful.'

They ate quickly and moved on, going carefully as the ground got rougher. Soon the overhanging cliffs, which made the gorge seem like a great gash in the earth, reared high and kept out the daylight. It was also hot and the air stifling. Dead trees and bushes showed up as eerie grey forms in the shadows. The men rode uneasily, eyes darting here and there and every movement in this dead world made them jumpy.

A vulture rose high in the sky further up the gorge, its great flapping wings causing an air current. Gus swore softly under his breath and looked over at Tom Kingsly, who was staring ahead. Gus knew by Tom's scowl that he knew what Gus knew. There were carcasses ahead.

They came upon the first one, already covered in ants. It was a yearling. Already its belly had been ripped open by the marauding birds, and its entrails hung out.

Gus dismounted and went to examine the body.

Its right leg was broken, caught up in a hole in the ground and it looked as if the whole herd had trampled it. There was a brand mark, LS, in a circle on its rump.

Gus returned to the others.

'Luke, it's one of yours,' he said tersely and mounted up again.

And so with a heavy heart they moved on. Soon they came to other bodies, all with signs of being trampled by other frightened horses.

They counted fifteen. It was a silent crew who moved on warily to the far end of the gorge, and there they were, the rest of the herd, milling about a great high needle of rock. Jesse Lowe gave a long low whistle.

'So Pa was right after all! Sometimes I thought it was all just a yarn.'

'Never mind your goddam, pa, Jesse.' Gus's voice was urgent. 'Let's get these animals out of this hell-hole! They're frantic for water and some of 'em look as if they're lame. Tom, can you get behind them? We've got to get 'em running round and round until that there leader makes for the back trail.'

'They'll panic, Gus!'

'Not if we do it right. Luke, you take the boys to the left and Kate, you go with Tom, and Jesse, you stick with me. Now gently does it. We're going to hum softly and we're going to ride around them until they start moving. Then, when they get going, Tom and Kate will wait on one side of the trail and me and Jesse will stand at the other side and see that they move on down. The others will follow behind and chase up the stragglers. Right?

They all nodded and went about their business. At first the small herd was nervous. The young stallions pricked up their ears, flung up their heads and swished their tails. Gradually, as they listened to the monotonous rhythm of the humming, they quietened down and began a slow walk following each other. They moved in a circle, growing closer together. In the centre of them was the towering needle of rock, still showing signs of smoke around its base, a reminder of the ancient past.

Carefully they watched the animals move ahead. Gus picked out the likely leader, a magnificent black stallion, taller than the rest, which had already got a following of mares. Gus waited, and when he came round again, Gus leapt from his mare and whacked her gently on the rump, saying softly:

'Go for him, Susie. Lead him down the trail!' Susie snorted and threw up her head as if she knew what to do. She galloped to the head of the bunch.

The black stallion snorted when he saw her ahead. She was usurping his lead role. He galloped after her and all the rest followed.

Jesse, wide-eyed, looked at Gus.

'What the hell you do that for?'

'Stop gabbing and give me a lift up! We follow and I'll pick Susie up further down the trail.' Gus sprang up behind Jesse and trotted along with the rest of the herd.

They found Susie, standing with ears pricked, looking back expectantly in-between two boulders. Gus laughed.

'There you are, Jesse! The perfect pard! That filly knows more than many humans. She's my best friend!'

'Aw, shit!' Jesse said disgustedly. 'She's just another goddammed horse!' Gus only smiled and said nothing.

The horses panicked a little when they smelled the blood of the corpses. They built up speed and everyone worried that they might stampede, but all the horses were tired and hungry and, most of all, thirsty. As they neared the junction they could smell green grass and water.

They swept on to the trail that led back into the valley and Gus felt a feeling of relief steal over him. It was good to be out of that cursed place. It was a shame about the casualties, and some of the horses would not be good enough for sale. It was a set back for the small ranchers but it could have been worse.

He was thinking these thoughts when Tom Kingsly and Kate joined him and Jesse. Tom took off his hat and mopped his sweating forehead.

'I hope to God we never have to chase after them again up in that canyon.'

'Well, it's up to you, Tom,' said Gus easily, 'Wildsmith could send his men out again and maybe next time see that *all* your horses are slaughtered. Who's to stop him?'

Tom looked at him steadily.

'Still want to go haring after him, and having a showdown? That way we get ourselves killed. You want that, eh?' He frowned. 'How do we know you aren't in league with the bastard? He's brought in professional gunmen before now. How do we know you aren't connected with him? Maybe all this is the build-up to something more serious. . . .'

'If that's the way you think, I'll be off. I don't need that kind of shit!' Gus spurred his mare into a gallop.

'Wait!' called Kate, upset at Tom's words, but Gus waved a hand to her and rode on. He was too angry with Kingsly. They could go ahead and settle their problem in their own way. Gus knew only too well how kowtowing to a bully only made him worse. The man he'd always reckoned to be his father had been a peaceful man and he'd died because of his belief.

The mare's stride lengthened and soon he was far down the trail that led back into the valley. Already he could see the Marshall ranch and, far beyond it, the cultivated land belonging to the other small ranchers. The view was magnificent, a paradise for those settling there. Plenty of grass and water and good fertile land for tilling. It was also perfect for the man who now coveted it and was turning paradise into hell.

Suddenly his eyes saw movement amongst the trees down by the river. He frowned and pulled out his field glasses for a better look. He saw a bunch of riders riding one behind the other in the shadow of the trees on the riverbank.

His reason told him they shouldn't be there. The menfolk of the three small ranches were back there, bringing the horses home, so these men must be bent on mischief.

He watched them for several minutes and saw that they were aiming for the trail in a slanting cross-country manoeuvre. He reckoned they would reach the trail at about sundown.

He put the glasses away in their case and turned off the trail. He knew exactly where he would hide out. There was a small promontory of rock which he'd noticed absent-mindedly as he'd passed by. He'd instinctively registered it as a good place for a hold-up. He reckoned this suspicious bunch would have to pass by if they were intent on raiding the returning herd.

'Come on, Susie, stretch those legs, girl, and let's get moving!' A gentle but firm dig in the ribs sent Susie into a long easy stride which she could keep up for hours.

The place was as he'd reckoned it would be, half-way up a hillside, part of a cluster of water-smooth boulders which had remained there long after the glacier which had brought them down had vanished. He led Susie into what was nearly a cave within which he would crouch and watch and wait.

He gave Susie a nosebag of oats from his saddle-bags and fished out a box of cartridges for the rifle in the boot. He loaded up and then looked to his Peacemaker. He was ready for action.

The sun was going down when he heard the herd coming. The smell of sweating horseflesh was on the wind. Gus reckoned they would bed down in the flat grassy stretch near the river, that was, if Tom Kingsly and the other men had any sense.

They could water the stock and let them feed and a couple of men could keep guard during what was known as the graveyard shift from midnight to sunrise.

He was right. The trotting horses were slowing down as Tom Kingsly, Kate and the rest of the men slowly encircled them. Heads lowered, they began to crop the grass while some of the outflankers made for the river to drink.

It was all as Gus had reckoned it would be. Soon, the camp-fire was blazing merrily. Every now and then a waft of coffee, would tickle Gus's nostrils. His guts grumbled. He could have done with a hot meal of fried bacon and panbread. He made do with what he had in his saddle-bags. He hunkered down and waited. There were men out there up to no good. He felt in his bones that they were waiting for the right time to strike.

He watched the two young men mount up and begin their nightly ride in opposite directions to ride around the settling herd. They would meet at the far side of the perimeter, have a few words and then move on. It was a very familiar procedure. At midnight they would be relieved and two others would take over for the next two hours and so it would be until dawn.

But this night would be different. Gus knew it in his bones. He shifted stiffly to make himself more comfortable and as he did so he saw the glint of a weapon amidst the trees away to the left. So that was where the bastards were hiding out!

He estimated his chances of being seen in the faint moonlight. Could he make his way to where the nighthawks would stop to talk and warn them what was about to happen?

He reckoned he could. The chances were that Wildsmith's men wouldn't attack until just before midnight, when the guard would be changed and all was quiet.

So, crouching low and keeping to the shadows, Gus moved forward in the slow deliberate way he'd been taught in the army during the Civil War. Patience and caution were the watchwords. The men rode twice round the herd before Gus was ready to intercept them.

He waited. Then he heard them coming from both directions. When they stopped to talk and have a quick drag at a cigarette, he silently approached and said softly,

'There's no need for panic, boys. It's me, Gus Strang.' One of them groped for his gun.

'What in hell. . . ?' began Luke Stratton's son.

'Sh . . . be quiet! Do you want to set off a stampede?' Gus asked in a harsh whisper.

'We thought you'd be miles away by now. Miss Kate was quite upset . . .'

'Never mind all that. You're being watched!'

46

The men stared at him in the moonlight. Gus looked grim. If this was a joke it was a bad one.

'Are you ringing our bells, mister?' one of them asked, half-angrily. 'Are you out to cause trouble because Tom Kingsly opened his big mouth?'

'Nope! You can take my word for it that there's a bunch of men out there in those trees yonder and they can only be Wildsmith's men, so what I want you to do is carry on as you are but when you work round to the campsite, warn the rest of your fellows what's happening.'

'While you ride off. If there's no one there, we'll look like a pair of idiots!'

'I'll be going nowhere. I'll be right here, waiting.'

The younger man scratched at a bristly chin.

'I'm beginning to think you mean what you say. What d'you think, Matt?'

Matt spat over his horse's neck.

'Sure. Could be. Why stick around here unless there's truth in what he says?'

'For Chris'sake, get moving! Warn Tom Kingsly to get everyone up and ready to ride the circle.'

'You mean for everyone to play nighthawk?'

'Yes, I mean just that. Those bastards out there will come trying to start a stampede. They must be stopped. A surprise attack on them will send them running!'

'But will they run?'

Gus laughed cynically.

'You bet they will. No man, no matter how well he's paid, will put his life on the line for a boss who stays well out of danger as Jed Wildsmith seems to do! Now get going. Tell Kingsly I'll be here and waiting!'

It was quite some time before Gus saw the first man approaching cautiously. Tom Kingsly must have been as sceptical as the two young men had been. But nevertheless, the extra man was a good sign.

He stepped out into the moonlight and held up his hand. It was Kingsly who dismounted beside him.

'Now what's all this nonsense about Wildsmith's men going to attack?'

'I saw them earlier. They're waiting in that stand of trees back there.' Gus pointed with his thumb in the direction from which they would come.

Kingsly looked and nodded.

'I'm sorry about what I said earlier.' He put out a hand and Gus grasped it. Gus smiled. 'So what do we do now?' Tom asked.

'Wait. Have everybody ready to guard the horses. They'll come charging down here hoping to set them stampeding again. But this time, I guess they'll be firing at us and not into the air.'

Kingsly looked at him with narrowed eyes.

'What makes you think that? Firing at us, I mean?'

'Because that's the logical thing to do. Get us looking after our own hides instead of watching the horses.'

'Sounds like you know what you're talking about!'

'Believe me, I do!' Gus thought back on the old days when he'd wrangled horses for old Nate Parker, the biggest and best horse-breeder in America. There'd been many raids on his horses and Gus knew every trick in the trade to foil would-be horse-thieves. But all that was past and done with. All he had left was the experience.

Kingsly went off to give orders and Kate joined Gus.

'When do you think they'll come?'

'Any time from now on but I wish you weren't here.'

'Why? I'm as good a shot as any man.'

'Because you're a woman and I don't want to be worrying about your hide when I'm trading shots with those varmints!' He turned away from her to go find his mare.

'Don't be ridiculous!' she shouted after him. 'What right have you to be worried?'

'No right, but I'd like to have the right!' He

strode away, leaving her heart beating fast, partly with anger and partly with a new excitement.

She cursed him under her breath. She didn't want to become entangled with any man. Once, years ago, she'd given her heart to a man and he'd laughed at her and thrown her love for him in her face. Never again did she want the humiliation of being rejected. She knew she was plain, homely was the word her father had used. She wasn't cut out to be any man's wife and the coming of Gus Strang was a dangerous experience.

She rode after Tom Kingsly. She would keep with the others and to hell with Gus Strang!

They came without warning. The bunch of riders had kept to the shadows cast by the trees until they were nearly upon the encampment. Then, with yells and shots, they charged, a line of men racing, like ghosts in the false dawn.

But there was a surprise waiting for them, as the resting horses started to mill about. Returned shots came thick and fast and the leader of the raiders was flung off his horse and rolled away to lie still.

Then all was confusion as the stallions and mares kicked up their heels and started to move. The line of raiders swerved, hidden behind the mass of bodies which were now gaining momentum as they got into their stride. Some of the yearlings lost their dams, panicked and galloped the wrong way and away from the trail.

Gus tried to get to the rear of the herd and come racing up behind the raiders. He shot one in the back before he knew he was being followed.

Then suddenly everything changed. Gus knew he'd been spotted. Three riders closed in on him. He leapt from Susie, smacked her smartly on the rump which made her break into a gallop, and dived for cover behind a boulder, firing as he did so, in the old army manoeuvre of dropping, rolling and firing.

He heard a yell and smiled. Another one less! He could hear screams and yells and the pounding of hoofs in the distance. The bastards had got the herd running. He concentrated on the two riders coming at him, zigzagging so that it was hard to get a bead on them, their own weapons firing indiscriminately. There was the splatter of bullets on the boulder beside him, punching out slivers of rock. One sliced a gash in his face.

It was evident they were experienced army veterans. Gus concentrated on the man nearest to him. He aimed at the horse's chest, something he hated to do, but he knew of old what the reaction would be. The horse stopped dead and crumpled. This gave Gus the chance he wanted. As the man catapulted forward, he took him in the throat.

Both man and horse collapsed in a heap.

Gus felt no elation at what he'd done but swivelled sharply to face the third man, who was coming up at an angle to get behind him. He aimed to fire but the trigger clicked on an empty barrel. He cursed, and as the young rider loomed over him he flung the empty gun full in the youth's face. Then, leaping to his feet, he caught the youth by the scruff of the neck as the horse galloped past, and brought him down with a thump.

But the fall hadn't knocked the boy out. His hands closed on Gus's neck and they rolled over and over with Gus gasping and straining to break the strangling hold.

He saw the savagery and the fear in the youth's eyes as they strained together. With teeth bared, the raider tried to bring pressure to Gus's larynx and Gus, heaving and twisting, managed to break free. He punched the man's mouth, breaking some teeth and, as he howled, Gus brought his knee up and caught the youth in the crotch.

Then, staggering to his feet, as he watched the man's agony, Gus loaded up his gun and pointed it squarely at the boy.

'I should kill you, you bastard!' The youth lay crouched, looking up, his eyes on the gun barrel pointing at his head. 'But I won't. You go back to your boss and tell him that Gus Strang is on his way to see him.'

'Does he know you?' the boy asked hoarsely.

'No, but he will before I've finished with him!' Gus turned away, ran lightly after his horse and mounted up. Then he leaned down over the youth who still lay on the ground. 'Ask him if he remembers Rosita Gonzalez.' As he rode away he heard the boy shout:

'Who's she?'

'He'll know,' Gus shouted back over his shoulder. He rode along the trail towards the scene of the recent mayhem. But the firing had ceased and the raiders were gone. He found Kate binding up Luke Stratton's arm and Jesse Lowe was loading up the body of one of his men on to his horse, his expression grim.

Tom Kingsly was missing; Gus presumed he was with the rest of the crew chasing up what was left of the herd.

He walked along the trail and examined several horses, mostly youngsters who hadn't been able to keep up with the rest and had got trampled. One lay with its head at an unnatural angle. Gus felt a bitter anger fill him. He hated cruelty and violent death for any animals. He was no hunter of animals . . . only of men.

He came back and mounted up. Kate watched

him with curious eyes, trying to read his mind.

'You all right?' he asked her brusquely.

'Yes.' Her hair had become loose. There was dirt on her face and her man's shirt was torn, showing an expanse of white shoulder. She felt uncomfortable under his gaze. She knew she looked dreadful. She would have been surprised if she'd known of his admiration of her.

'You can manage OK without me?'

'Of course!' but she sounded surprised at the question. 'Aren't you coming back to the ranch?'

'No. I'm moving on.'

'But . . . but why the hurry? Is it because of what Tom Kingsly said? We do trust you, you know.'

'No. It's private business. Nothing to do with you or anyone else.'

'Oh! I'm sorry I asked! I didn't mean to pry! So it's goodbye then?' She sounded offended at what she thought of as a snub.

'I'm sorry. I've been clumsy, but this is hardly the time to think of anyone's feelings. I came into this country for a purpose and now I've got to get on with it. So it's goodbye for now.'

'You'll come back?'

He looked at her enigmatically.

'Maybe. It's all in the lap of the gods!'

THREE

Jed Wildsmith raised his cane and struck the desk, glaring at the black-suited man standing before him.

'Why wasn't I told Kit Childs was dead? Why didn't you tell me his widow was selling her holding? Goddammit! I pay you well enough to keep me informed about what's going on, on the range! I can't do all the work myself! You're incompetent and a fool! I've a good mind to kick you out of that office I own and cut you adrift! Now what are we going to do about it, eh?'

'But . . . but I told you . . . it's already sold! All done and signed. There's nothing—'

'Of course there's something we can do,' bellowed Wildsmith. 'We can do what we've done before. Threaten the feller, harass him if he's stubborn! I want that land!'

'The matter was never in my hands, Jed,' quavered the lawyer who was visibly trembling at the onslaught of passion his news had brought forth. 'It was all done by a city slicker. The widow was approached privately and the deal was done without the help of the lawyer. It was the man's lawyer who did the paperwork—'

'Jesus H. Christ! Don't you lawyers live in each other's pockets? You should have known!'

Cyrus G. Lovel sighed. If any other man gave him this kind of shit, he would have quickly put him in his place, but Jed Wildsmith was a man of a different calibre. Besides, Jed knew too much about Cyrus's rift with the law many years ago and never let Cyrus forget it. One trod on eggshells when around Jed.

'Look, I'll see what I can do. All I know is that he's called A.S. Gonzalez and he's a Texan.'

Wildsmith snorted. 'Some half-breed Mex, no doubt. But why the hell should he want a place in Montana? He'll be well out of his territory.'

'I heard from one of the widow's hands that he breeds horses. That he's got a way with animals and has the wildest stallion eating out of his hand in a matter of days.'

'Huh! Sounds a useful man to know. A pity such a man wasn't looking for a job. My present wrangler knows shit!'

Cyrus watched him out of narrowed eyes. The old man was visibly calming down. The talk of horses had done the trick. Jed Wildsmith might be an all-round bastard but he genuinely loved his horses.

The old man reached into the humidor on the desk for a cigar. He lit it, blowing blue smoke into the air. Cyrus's nose twitched at the rich aroma, but Jed, the mean old scumbag, did not offer him one. Cyrus cursed inwardly as the craving for tobacco nearly overcame him.

Jed Wildsmith's shrewd old eyes twinkled amusedly for a moment. He recognized Cyrus's reaction and played on it. He could reduce the man to nothing more than a puppet any time he wanted. Sometimes he wondered whether Cyrus was aware of why he was never offered a cigar. Cyrus would put it down to his, Jed's, meanness.

Jed leaned forward and pointed a finger at Cyrus.

'You keep a look-out for this Gonzalez feller and bring him here. I want to talk to him. You hear? Do what you do best! Put your dogs on his trail! But bring him to me . . . or else!'

Gus Strang rode cross-country, admiring the views and thinking about his eventual meeting with his father. Although brought up in Texas, he had a feeling of affinity with these lush rolling hills, the forests and the flat pastures. His nostrils wrinkled pleasantly at the spicy scent of pines, good herbage and the sweet smell of mountain air. He felt invigorated and strong and, above all, he felt as if he was coming home.

He smiled to himself as he thought of Jed Wildsmith's reaction when he knew that a small homestead had been bought from under his nose.

Gus's first reaction on hearing the news of his father from his dying mother was to hire a Pinkerton man to find out all about Jed Wildsmith and the Montana country. The detective had done his job well, and it had become clear what kind of man his father was. Also, the Pinkerton man had reported on the death of Kit Childs. The gossip had been that Jed Wildsmith would soon take over. There had been much grumbling from folk in the little township close by. Jed Wildsmith owned part of the town. He owned the sheriff and the mayor and now he had a stranglehold on the town itself.

Gus's eyes had glistened when he'd heard of Childs's death. He had instructed a lawyer from Seattle, at great expense, to approach the widow and make her an offer she couldn't refuse. It had worked. Gus had bought a small ranch unseen.

Now he was curious to see the ranch and the

country he now owned. All he knew of it was that it was good horse-breeding country.

As he rode along he planned his immediate future. He would make for the ranch and settle in. He was taking on Kit Childs's men, three of them, and they were caring for the small herd that Mrs Childs had thrown in for luck.

Then, when all his affairs were in order, he would tackle Jed Wildsmith and take his revenge on behalf of his mother.

He wondered just what that revenge would be. He shrugged the thought away. This thing would settle itself. He would play it by ear. It all depended on what reaction Jed Wildsmith showed when confronted by a son now forty years old.

The sun was lowering in the sky when he chanced on a small hamlet. A crooked board, crudely painted with the words LONGHORN CREEK, 351 SOULS, with the one crossed out and a 0 in its place, stood by the dirt trail leading into town. A dog barked as he approached and a man in a stained apron appeared at the door of a small store, drying his hands on a dirty towel.

He looked expectantly at Gus and his expression changed to one of disappointment as he saw the lone rider. Gus put up a hand and reined in his mare.

'Howdy, mister! I'm looking for the KC ranch.

Can you point me in the right direction?'

The storeman looked Gus and the mare over and then spat in the dust.

'You be a stranger in these parts,' he said judiciously. 'If you've come from over by Johnson's Hollow, you've passed it!'

Gus shrugged.

'I wouldn't know Johnson's Hollow if I fell into it!'

The man spat again.

'You've ridden over the big M ranch. The KC is smack bang next to it. It's a wonder you didn't run into some of Kate Marshall's boys.'

'Kate Marshall?'

'Yeah, your nearest neighbour. But what you want at the KC? Kit's up and died and his widow's sold up and left. If you're looking for a job, you'll get no joy at the KC. They're waiting for their new boss to arrive.'

'Yes, I know the situation.'

'You do?'

Gus nodded, quieting Susie, who was becoming restive.

'You mean you're. . . ?'

'You might say that.'

'Then you're this Mex feller, A.S. Gonzalez?' Then he frowned. 'You ringing my bell, mister? You don't look like no Mex to me!'

'Why should I look like a Mex?'

'Because of the name, mister! We're looking for some Mex to come horning in, in this here town. That's what!'

'Well, I'm sorry to disappoint you but I'm him. Now what about selling me a few vittles to see me on my way?'

At that, the man brightened.

'Now that's more like it! You'll be my first customer of the day.'

'So you don't do much business?'

'Nope! Just the homesteaders. Jed Wildsmith's fancy store run by the lick-ass mayor takes all the main trade of the big boys. They've even imported silk for women's dresses. I don't know what the world's coming to! When I was young, women and girls were lucky to have a Sunday going-to-church gown made of good stout cotton! Now the women-folk are getting big ideas. He's even selling them washboards so they can wash clothes at home instead of in the river!' He spat again disgustedly and coughed wheezily. 'Well? Have you a list, mister? Or are you coming in to see what I've got?'

Gus dismounted and hitched Susie to the hitching rail in front of the store. He entered and was hit by the mixed smells of coffee, onions and coal-oil and many more odours he wasn't sure of. It took him a few minutes for his eyes to become used to the gloom. The storeman skipped behind his counter and waited.

'Well?'

Gus took a look around. There was everything a settler would need, from sacks of flour and dried beans, drums of coffee and packets of brown sugar, jars of molasses and tins of peaches to bedrolls, blankets, pots and pans, checked flannel shirts of all colours, riding-boots, canvas pants and red-flannel long johns with vests to match. There were bolts of calico, gingham and fine white linen and, hanging on hooks, a selection of lamps, brooms, pickaxes and hoes and all the tools a man would want on a ranch.

'I see you've got plenty to choose from.'

'Yeah, but not what the womenfolk want these days. They've gone all lah-di-dah. China pots instead of earthenware and brass clocks, and Jed Wildsmith figures on bringing in any damn thing a woman craves! That's how he stays on top, the king of the range. He gets the women behind him!'

'They don't object to his riding roughshod over the small ranchers?'

'Nary a bit of it! The townsfolk couldn't care less for the little ranchers. They're all busy licking Wildsmith's ass! Now what you want? Coffee? Flour?'

'Yes, and a jar of molasses. I'm partial to it, and

a small sack of beans and some of those chilli peppers.'

The storeman talked as he gathered Gus's order together. Gus wanted a couple of shirts and some new long johns. He'd worn holes in those he was wearing with all his hard riding and he indulged himself with some new thick socks to stop the blisters on his feet.

The storeman licked his lips as Gus counted out the dollar bills. The stranger sure was the new owner of the KC! He hadn't seen so much ready cash in months. Most folk bought and put their goods on his slate, to be paid when they'd sold a crop or a cow or horse. This man was worth cultivating.

'Would you care for a drink before you go?' the storeman asked casually. 'I've got some good rotgut whiskey in the back.'

Gus smiled and for the first time, Lenny Beale saw that look in Gus's eyes which he recognized. This man had killer's eyes, the same cold, slate-blue eyes like . . . he couldn't quite bring to mind, just whose eyes they reminded him of. He gave a sickly smile in return. It was as if this stranger knew what Lenny had in mind.

'I don't mind if I do!'

Lenny was pleased. For the moment he forgot the uncomfortable impression he'd received. He ushered his visitor into the room at the back of the store. Half of it was a storeroom and the rest was his bedroom and living-space. A pot-bellied stove took up part of the wooden floor and beside it was a barrel with a tap. Lenny found a couple of mugs and poured the whiskey for both of them.

They raised their glasses together and drank. Then Lenny offered Gus the only chair, by the stove, and he sat on his narrow bed.

Gus sat down and spread his legs, the alcohol coursing a fiery path through him. It tasted good.

'You sell much of this?' He held up the mug. Lenny's head bobbed up and down excitedly. He was sure he'd got a sale.

'Yes. A backwoodsman I know has a still and brings in several barrels at a time every few months. It's one thing Jed Wildsmith can't beat me with!'

'The next time you get a consignment, keep me two barrels and I'll collect and pay cash!'

Lenny filled up Gus's mug. The big man could sure sup his drink and not turn a hair. He'd seen men yelling Indian war whoops on one mug. This feller didn't seem affected at all! Lenny's respect for Gus grew rapidly. He looked up to a man who could hold his liquor.

Suddenly there were loud footsteps on the wooden flooring in the store and an angry voice was yelling for Lenny. The door burst open and a tall, rangy grey-haired man was standing there. But what astonished Lenny was the speed with which his new friend swivelled round to meet the newcomer and the way the long-barrelled Peacemaker jumped into his hand. Lenny's eyes travelled upward and he was shocked to see the cold eyes glittering with an intensity which made the newcomer pause in the doorway.

'Hold it!' barked Gus. The grey-haired man's hands lifted above his shoulders, all anger drained from him. 'You're lucky, mister. When a man barges in like that I have a notion to shoot first and ask questions afterwards! Now what's the trouble?' But he did not put away his gun. He looked from the man to Lenny. 'You know this *hombre*?'

'Yes. Meet our sheriff, Ethan Fry. Ethan, I don't know what your beef is, but I reckon before you spout out your grievance, you'd better meet the new owner of the KC.'

Ethan Fry stared at Gus. So this burly man with the curly beard and the look of the devil in his eyes was the man his boss, Jed Wildsmith, was spitting blood over! Christ! He had enough on his plate without running into this guy!

Reluctantly he spoke, seeing that Gus was remaining silent and vigilant.

'Hi! Pleased to meet you.' He held out his hand. Gus ignored it. For a long moment the hand hung there and then Ethan flushed and groped for a cigarette, looking at Lenny for support.

Gus stood up, stretched and then, thrusting the Peacemaker back into its holster, gathered up his groceries, gesturing to Lenny to help him with the rest of his purchases.

'If you give me a hand, mister, I'll be on my way and you can deal with this here . . . er . . . gent.' He spoke contemptuously.

Ethan Fry swore under his breath but something in the stranger's eyes warned him to back off.

Lenny took his time to help Gus load up in the two saddle-bags and strap on an old sack Lenny had found for him to carry the rest of his goods.

'Thanks for the order, mister. I'm sure grateful,' Lenny said softly. Gus glanced at him as he forked his mare.

'I'll be back.' He rode away at an easy canter.

Ethan Fry came to stand beside beside Lenny. They both watched Gus ride away, growing smaller in the distance.

'Nice mare,' Ethan opined. 'Where did he come from?'

'Rode in from the direction of the Marshall place. Wanted to know where the KC was situated.'

'And you told him?'

'Yes. Why shouldn't I? He also paid cash for what he got. Not like some folk!' He glared at the sheriff. Ethan Fry looked angry but said nothing. He had something else on his mind. Eventually he said softly,

'There was something strange about that feller.'

'You felt it too?'

The men looked at each other. Ethan Fry reached for a chaw of tobacco.

'Yep. Killer's eyes, that's what he had. He would have shot me without hesitation if I'd given him an excuse and thought nothing of it.' Ethan bit on the tobacco and chewed thoughtfully. 'His eyes reminded me . . .' He stopped and then went on, 'Aw hell, it sounds ridiculous but he had eyes kind of like Wildsmith's. He's got the same look, the bleak dead stare and by God, the same goldarn slatey-grey. I never trusted a man with eyes that colour.'

'Is that why you keep in with Wildsmith? Because you're frightened of him?' Now Lenny was mocking. 'Why you become a lick-ass?'

The punch caught Lenny unawares. He was slammed up against a shelf of Dr Langton's Cure-all medicine bottles which cascaded on to the floor around him. Lenny shook his head, felt his jaw and then, wading in, caught Ethan Fry a wallop that rattled his ears.

Ethan Fry backed off. He wasn't a barroom brawler. He was more used to showing his authority with a gun in his fist.

'Now, now, Lenny . . . I could arrest you for assault, so take it easy, will ya?'

'Assault, you low-down ass-licking bastard! You hit me first!'

'You asked for it! I don't take kindly to being accused of no ass-licking. If I didn't know you well, I'd put a shot into your knee-caps, by God I would!'

'Get out of here! Go on! If you don't want to buy something, you have no right to be in here! Look what you've done! Two bottles broken! If you had any good in you, you'd pay for them!'

The sheriff grunted.

'Jesus, Lenny, you know I don't get a pay-check good enough to pay for breakages! Stick a couple of cents on the other bottles. You'll soon get the cash back that way!'

'Aw, just get out of here! Think yourself a sheriff? A skunk would do a better job than you do! So go and jump into the horse trough before I throw this bottle at you!' Lenny grabbed one of the bottles and started to swing it round and round.

Ethan Fry gave him a dirty look.

'I'm going and you can be sure I'll tell Wildsmith that he can't have his whiskey until after the new feller has got his! That will make his day!'

He dived for the door as the bottle left Lenny's hand. It crashed against the lintel and smashed. The noxious smell of snake-oil mixed with bitter herbs filled the store.

Ethan Fry peered around the door.

'Make that three extra cents a bottle, Lenny.'

He went away chuckling.

Gus rode on until the shadows had lengthened and a three-quarter moon was bright in the sky. He could have stayed overnight in the small hamlet but he was always uneasy in rented rooms, for sometimes the beds were lousy, the blankets smelling of stale bodies and the striped ticking-covered pillows lacked pillowcases and were greasy from many heads. Several times in the past he'd picked up both lice and fleas from such places. He much preferred sleeping under the stars.

He soon coaxed a small fire to burn. First he'd found several flat stones and built them up in a ring, so that the fire itself was contained. Then he used dry dead wood which gave off little flame. Soon he was crouching over it, feeling its warmth and balancing a blackened coffee-pot with some of his new coffee on to boil. He was camping near a small stream amidst a stand of trees. He found a stale hunk of bread in one of his saddle-bags and a slice of pickled pork. It wasn't much but it staved off his hunger. He was used to going long hours without food. It would serve until he came to his ranch house.

Sitting content and watching the small flames dancing upwards he felt strangely relaxed. This mountainous land of Montana called to something deep inside him. It was as if his roots were already striking down into the rich earth. Now he knew why the Indians fought so hard to keep their land. It was something that bound them fast and they couldn't help themselves. He knew that once he had settled on his own land he would fight to the death to keep it.

He was becoming drowsy when he first heard the noise in the undergrowth. At once, he was wide awake and reaching for his gun. All senses alert, he waited and watched and gradually squirmed his way until he was away from the fire and hiding under a bush.

He waited and watched.

Then he saw movement amongst the trees and debated with himself, should he fire first and ask questions afterwards? It could be one of the Marshall woman's men investigating his fire. He remembered the three men. He couldn't fire without warning, that would be murder.

Then, to his surprise, a young mustang stepped out of the trees and into the moonlight. Gus relaxed, put his gun back in his holster and gave a low whistle. He saw the horse's ears twitch and lift.

Slowly, Gus got to his feet and moved into the open. The horse, which looked to be a four-year-old, nickered. Slowly Gus took several steps forward, speaking softly with a sing-song lilt that he knew was soothing to a nervous animal.

'Come on, boy, I'm not going to hurt you.' He waited and the young stranger took several cautious steps forward. Then Susie whinnied and threw up her head, for she'd smelled a strange scent. The horse trotted over to her, and Gus followed. He ran his hand along the animal's back and down his rump.

Gus saw that he was a stallion. Perhaps that was why he'd come to them, because he was attracted to Susie's scent.

'Well, well,' Gus muttered, 'you must be one of the herd that got away yesterday.' He felt a dried crust of blood on the animal's right flank. So the beast had been grazed by a bullet and frightened into bolting away from the others.

It was clear that this stallion was partially broken-in. He wondered whether Kate Marshall owned him or did he belong to one of the neighbours? He was a loss to whomever he belonged to. He was a good specimen and would make a good stud animal in time. There was nothing else for it, he would have to take him along and return him to Kate Marshall when he had the time.

He dug into the small bag of oats that he carried for Susie and gave the stallion a measure of feed in his hat. That seemed to steady the animal and Gus knew he wouldn't stray far from them.

Then Gus rolled himself in his blanket and settled down for the rest of the night.

He slept late and the sun was well risen when he a woke up with a start, only to find the young stallion snuffling at his leather oat-bag.

'Hey there! Now don't be greedy, boyo. There's plenty of grass around so leave that bag alone!' The horse's head came up. He pricked his ears at Gus's voice and took a couple of dancing steps backwards. Gus grinned. He liked the spunkiness of his new friend. Now he lay and looked at the clean-cut lines of him in the morning light. Gee, good strong withers, muscled legs that denoted a good stayer, a noble head and a glistening chestnut coat, meaning he was special to someone. This feller was being groomed as a stud and was worth a year's groceries!

For a while he lay watching him. It was a tempting thought to hide him away and train him himself. Gee, what a thought! Then he shook his head. No good getting in bad with whomever owned the beast if ever he was found out.

Men had been shot for horse-stealing.

He rolled out of his blanket, stood up and stretched. It would be good to splash in that stream and wash the dirt and sweat of many weeks from his body. He would take the advantage and wear a pair of his new red-flannel long johns with a vest to match. He could dry himself on his raggy pants before tossing them away. Yes, he would have a leisurely clean-up before eating.

The stream was clear and refreshingly cold enough to make Gus jump up and down and splash around like some half-grown kid. The water cleared away the last dregs of sleep and he ducked and dived and relaxed. His spirits rose. He hoped this stream ran past his own ranch house, or a stream something like it.

The stream was waist-deep and ran leisurely over a sandy bottom scattered with rounded pebbles. He saw small fish darting here and there and was tempted to stay and catch a few for his breakfast but, having no hooks or bait, he knew it would take up too much time. He could fish later as and when he wanted, when he was settled in his new home. It was a pleasure yet to come.

Finally, having exhausted his early kicking and splashing, he allowed himself to float and drift and dream a little. The gentle current carried him at least fifty yards from his pile of clothing. The sounds the rippling stream made were hypnotic. He could have been in paradise.

Then suddenly he heard a sound that froze his guts. It was the sound of a woman's laughter. His feet hit the gravel and he turned to face the sound. The water streamed off his broad shoulders and ran down his hairy chest. His shock of hair straggled on to his shoulders.

'What in hell. . . ?' he began as he looked at Kate Marshall. She was wearing men's pants, a red checked shirt and a man's broad-brimmed and very dirty Stetson on her head, hiding her hair. But what was most impressive of all, she was holding a rifle with a business-like air at his chest.

'So, you're a rustler too, Mr Strang. I thought you said you had business to attend to. I see it was the business of rustling. The law says I should shoot a rustler.'

'Now listen here, lady—'

'No! You listen to me! You're one of Wildsmith's imported gunmen, aren't you? You came pretending to help me. God knows why but I'm on to you now. Yes sir!'

'You're on the wrong track, Miss Marshall. I'm no rustler. If you're referring to that there stallion, he came into my camp last night. You can see for yourself he's not tied in any way. He could have gone whenever he pleased.'

'You must have done something to make him stay!'

'I fed him some oats. He looked forlorn and then he took a shine to Susie and stayed with her. Blame her, not me. Is he yours, by the way?'

'Yes.'

'Then you should thank me for keeping him close by, not rail at me like some spinsterish shrew!'

She took a deep breath, shocked at his words.

'Spinsterish shrew! I'll have you know . . .' Then she stopped uncomfortably.

'Yes?' asked Gus curiously.

'Oh, to hell with you! Just get out of that freezing water so that we can talk properly.'

Gus eyed his clothes further upstream.

'I'm a long way from my clothes.'

'Well? What are you waiting for? Just walk back upstream. I don't mind waiting.'

Gus, feeling a fool, struggling clumsily against the rush of water, finally made it. He turned to the bank and with horror, saw that Kate had followed silently, holding her horse by the bridle. They glared at each other. Kate spoke.

'Well, when are you coming out?'

Gus was shivering. His ass and legs were beginning to freeze.

'Any time now.'

'Then get on with it!'

'If you were a lady I shouldn't have to ask you to turn your back!'

'I'm no lady!'

Gus shrugged. 'I'm not disputing that! I've never met a woman less like a lady!'

'Thank you!' The words were growled.

'So, I'll just have to treat you as a man if that's what you are!'

She stiffened and bridled at the insult but stood her ground, lifting her chin and gritting her teeth. This man was insufferable.

Then, slowly, Gus waded ashore, standing straight and tall. He had never been exceptionally proud of his body but he was all man and had proved it many times in the past. Now, as her roving eyes took him all in he suddenly grinned.

'Satisfied?' She had the grace to blush and only then turned away while he slowly shook out his new underwear and dressed.

He threw his ragged pants into a bush, picked up his dirty vest and sauntered over to her.

'Now that we're more than just strangers passing in the night, might I ask you to eat breakfast with me? It's only stale bread and the remains of pickled pork but you're welcome to it!'

Her lips tightened at his mockery.

'I have my own food, thank you, and I've eaten already.'

'Well, at least you can share a cup of coffee with me while we talk. It *was* talk you said you wanted? Nothing else?'

Again she flushed. It made her look younger and prettier and, for a second or two, Gus felt his reaction. It had been quite some time since he'd slept with a woman.

Down, boy, he mentally told himself, this woman's not for taking. He took his mind off her as he busied himself on building up the nearly dead embers of his fire while she took his coffee-pot and filled it from the stream.

Then, when the water had boiled and the coffee had been added and the aroma filled the air, Gus squatted and brought out his stale bread and the remains of his pork. She eyed it with disfavour.

'Is that really all you've got?'

'Uh huh.' He broke off pieces of bread. It was hard but he could soak it in his coffee.

'For God's sake, throw it away! I can see green mould on it! Here, you can have some of mine.'

She got up from the fire and walked across to her tethered horse. On the way, Gus saw that the mustang which had found him trotted up to her and stood nuzzling her, while she patted his head. Lucky beast!

Then she strode back to him with a sack which had hung from the pommel of her saddle. She threw it down to him.

'Here, take what's left. There's cold beef and the pan bread's fresh. I made it for my breakfast.'

'You're sure? I wouldn't want to deprive you.'

'You were the means of me finding my stallion, so it's a fair exchange. Besides, I don't have to ride all over the range looking for him. I can go on home.' She looked as if she might leave without having some coffee.

'You in a hurry? I thought you would have some coffee.'

'Well, if you press me.'

'Oh, I'll press you all right . . . anytime!' and he enjoyed seeing her face redden again. Gosh, she was even prettier. Maybe it was because he hadn't seen a female under forty for a long spell.

He wondered how old she was.

She wasn't a spinster as such, but she was past the nubile age for young females to marry. He wondered about her life here on the range. Her cooking was good. That was in her favour.

She watched him enjoy the roasted beef and the fresh bread. He sighed when he'd had his fill.

'I'll keep the rest for later,' he said and belched satisfyingly. He could have done with a fart but thought better of letting rip, even if she reckoned she wasn't a lady.

Then, on his third cup of coffee he figured he had nothing to lose if he asked the question which had been on the tip of his tongue ever since he'd waded out of the stream.

'Well, what did you think?'

'About what?'

'About me. You know, when I came out of the stream and you took a darn good look.'

'Jesus! What a thing to ask a lady!'

'A lady wouldn't have looked so it don't signify. I'm asking you as a woman.'

She frowned and tried to look serious but he saw her lips curve at the corners.

'I've seen better . . .'

'Oh? Have you?'

'If you'd let me finish, I was going to say I'd seen better tackle on a yearling foal. But as a man . . .'

'Yes?'

'I can't give an opinion as I haven't seen any other men to compare!'

Gus threw his tin mug down in mock frustration. Secretly he was pleased she hadn't played tag with the cowhands.

'Of all the goldarn aggravating females, you sure beat 'em all! You have the nerve to look at a feller as if he's a prize stallion and then you haven't the guts to follow through and tell me what you really think. I give up!'

'Does it really matter what I think? After all, you're a stranger in these parts and it's likely I'll never see you again after today. Or are you so full of yourself that you have to be flattered at all times? If you want to know . . .' and now she paused for effect, 'I think you're . . .'

'Yes?'

'What the Mexicans would say was a *macho caballero*. Is that good enough?'

'I wanted to know what *you* thought, not a pesky Mex!'

She shrugged and got to her feet collecting her war bag. She stared down at him before turning away and then said over her shoulder.

'I agree with the Mex!' She turned and ran, caught the young stallion by the mane and led him to her horse, where she untied her lariat from its hook on her saddle. She made a makeshift bridle and tossed it over his head. Then Gus watched her vault on to her horse in one lithe movement. The woman was sure some mover. He was smiling as she rode past him, giving him a wave and an impish grin. He waved back and he still had a silly grin on his face when she was long gone.

FOUR

It had been a long haul.Gus had taken two wrong turns before he found his ranch. Finally he'd come across a youth rounding up a couple of mares with foals running at their heels. Gus saw the KC brand on the mares' rumps.

'You from the KC,' he asked jokily, 'or are you rustling horses?'

The youth stared, not realizing Gus was joking.

'And who wants to know?' He spoke truculently. He didn't like smartass strangers.

'I'm looking for the KC ranch. I suppose it's here somewhere?'

'Yeah, but the boss is dead and his missus has sold up and we're minding the stock, so I don't know what your interest is.'

'You don't need to know!' Now Gus's tone was

cold. 'I asked you a civil question. Am I on the right track?'

The youth nodded sulkily.

'I'm driving these critters back to the ranch, so if you help me, you'll get there sooner rather than later.'

'Good. Now what do I call you?'

'Well, if it's any of your business, I'm Skip. What's your moniker, mister?'

'Gus Strang, and you can call me Mr Strang. Right?'

'If you say so, *Mr Strang*.' The youth stressed his name.

Skip might be sulky but he knew how to handle horses and Gus knew the boy was worth whatever Kit Childs had paid him. But it wasn't fair to tell him he was his new boss until he had lined up the other members of the crew.

They slowly came to the top of a rise and now joined a well-used track. Now, for the first time, Gus saw his new home. It lay in a slight hollow amidst a lush green pasture bounded by a thick frame of pine trees. He paused to take in the view. Kit Childs had chosen his location well.

Good flat land, with room for corral and outbuildings, nothing elaborate but workmanlike, a small bunkhouse and presumably a cookhouse close by, for smoke billowed from a metal chimney.

The house itself was small but adequate with a veranda facing south and a stream which ran a few hundred yards away. He could see a ploughed-up square of land like a patchwork, which presumably was the main source of the fresh-food supply. Probably the widow had spent her days hoeing and raking while the menfolk looked after the cattle and horses.

There were few cattle but Gus already knew that she kept one milk-cow for the house and several pigs. The information had come at the time of the sale.

Now he was keen to get down there and meet his crew.

An old man with a bald head and a limp came out of the cookhouse, wiping his hands on his dirty apron. A younger, but middle-aged man came out of the barn and stared as the mares and foals, followed by the two men, galloped down the straight and into the yard.

'Whoa there,' shouted the man from the barn. 'What in hell's got into you, Skip? You'll have those mares charging yon fence and the foals breaking their necks to get to 'em if you don't watch out!'

Skip pulled up with a jerk at the reins and his horse reared, kicking up the dust of the yard and making the man standing at the barn door yell fit to bust a gut.

'Gee, Jack, I don't know what got into the critters! I can only think they want to get back to the rest of 'em.'

'Who's the feller riding with you?'

'A guy called Strang. He likes to be called mister!' There was scorn in the boy's voice.

'Huh! Wise guy, eh? He has no business setting foot on this here place! Didn't you tell him to skedaddle?'

'Yeah, but it was no use. He said he had business here.'

Jack frowned. 'Then I'll just go and check him out.' He strode across the yard to where Gus, on his horse, was looking about him and assessing what he saw.

'Hi, there, stranger! What can I do for you?.'

'More like what I can do for you!'

'Oh? And what *can* you do for me?' Jack's eyes roved over Gus and the horse, taking in the stuffed saddle-bags, the bedroll, the condition of the black mare and her smooth sleek lines showing stamina and speed. Then his eyes stopped at the holster about the big man's waist. He could bet on it, it was a powerful Peacemaker. Then his eyes slid over the Spencer repeating rifle in the boot. The man was an arsenal on four legs. He looked up at Gus with more respect.

'Just who are you, mister?'

'I'm Gus Strang, known as A.S. Gonzalez. Know the name?'

'Hell, yes, I know the name but you're no Mex!'

Gus shrugged. 'Nevertheless, I own that name. I'm your new boss!'

The man called Jack looked sceptical. He rubbed his chin.

'Now what makes me think you're telling the truth, mister? Any doggone shyster could ride in and give us that spiel. You're not even a Mex!'

Gus smiled, reached into his vest pocket and pulled out a sheaf of official-looking papers.

'Can you read?'

'Yeah, I can read.'

'Then take a look at these. I can also tell you that the southern boundary of my two thousand, three hundred and fifty-seven acres is bounded by Potter's Gyll, and Totem Peak is close by. Isn't that right?'

Jack scratched his head while peering at the official deed.

'Yeah, I guess you're right, mister ... er ... boss.' Then he looked puzzled as he handed back the papers. 'But why call yourself Gonzalez when you also call yourself Strang?'

Gus looked at him steadily. If he was to live with these men they should know part of the truth.

'My ma was a Mex called Rosita Gonzalez.'

'And your pa was a man called Strang?' Jack chuckled.

'You might say that.'

Jack's face creased in an amused smile. He held out his hand and said bluntly:

'You're a bastard. Join the club, boss! I'm a true legitimate bastard myself!' They both laughed while the others looked on wide-eyed.

Then Jack turned to the others.

'Come closer, guys. This is your new boss, A.S. Gonzalez, known as Mr Strang.'

'Gus. Just call me Gus.'

'Gus it is then, boss. Now you know Skip, and I'm Jack Jones, Jones being as good a name as any! And the old coot over there is Ikey, the best biscuit-maker in the business!' Then he turned confiden- tially to Gus. 'Ikey was our wrangler until he got his leg smashed and he became our cook, but Bessie, that is Mrs Childs, always cooked for Kit. We live and eat over in the bunkhouse.' Then he looked anxious. 'I suppose you *are* keeping us on?'

'Of course! I'm depending on you all! There'll be no changes unless there's a good reason. You guys know the country and will have to keep me right. I'll be depending on you all, and, if I may, I'd like to join you in the bunkhouse for my meals. Is that all right with you fellers?'

The men looked at each other and it was Ikey who spoke up. 'It's all right with us, boss. It's the first time a boss has supped with us and we're mighty pleased.' Then he went on, 'I think I can speak for us all when I say we're goldarn grateful to be kept on. I been here nigh on forty years, man and boy, ever since Kit Childs dug his first post-hole and Jack here has been with us . . . how long, Jack?'

'Fifteen years come Thanksgiving.'

'And Skip here rode in five years ago. So you see, boss, we'd have no place to go if you gave us our marching orders.'

'You needn't worry, Ikey. There's a place here as long as you want to stay. Now I'll get myself inside and look about, and Ikey, there's some staples on my horse. They'll come in handy in the cookhouse.' Gus, feeling a little emotional, strode away towards the main house. He wanted to be alone to savour his new home.

Skip took Susie and held her while Ikey unloaded the saddle-bags and sorted the foodstuffs. He exclaimed delightedly at the coffee and flour and all the rest. Jack went back to the barn much lighter-hearted than he'd been for a long time. Now the boss could deal with any trouble that came along from Jed Wildsmith when he heard the news that the new owner had claimed his ranch.

Gus gazed around at the long narrow room. It was still furnished with rough, handmade furniture, just the bare necessities, like a table, two upright chairs, two rockers and a chest which Gus suspected might hold blankets. There was a dresser with shelves and drawers, where rough blue-and-white china was displayed. Now the china was thick with dust. There was a rough shelf on the wooden wall with several books and a couple of jars which Gus reckoned Bessie Childs had used for flowers. There was a gunrack holding an ancient shotgun which Bessie evidently hadn't wanted. There were marks of oil around the other wooden hooks which denoted that Kit had had several different kinds of guns.

He opened a door and stepped into a small square hall. Two doors led from it. One door opened into a long narrow bedroom and the other opened on to a storeroom, in which several interesting items were still there; one of them was a tin bath, so Bessie Childs hadn't relied on washing in the creek close by. There was a pile of colourful blankets lying on a packing-case. Gus looked under them and saw that the box was filled with a feather quilt. He took a closer look about him and saw many objects that could only mean that Bessie Childs had hoped at one time to be a mother. Poor Bessie. She'd never had a child.

So this bedroom had been turned into a store-room. He wondered why she'd left everything. Maybe it was too painful to pack it all up and take it with her.

He shut the door. The blankets might prove useful but the rest would stay where it was.

Then Ikey came in, his bald head glistening with sweat. He'd been cooking over a hot fire.

'Boss . . . er . . . Gus, I got hot biscuits and stew all ready, and Jack and Skip are waiting to eat. Will you come now?'

'Sure. My guts are rumbling. No need to keep the guys waiting.'

The bunkhouse was one long room. Half of it was taken by two sets of bunkbeds and the rest was filled by a long table with two benches. The rest of the walls held hooks for clothes and a couple of shelves which held a bible, a shaving-mirror, several cups and plates and a few personal items. A pot-bellied stove belched out heat and smoke and there was a scattering of wood-ash at its feet.

'Sorry about the mess,' Ikey said. 'If we'd known earlier about you eating with us, we would have cleaned up.' He looked pointedly at Skip's dirty laundry lying by his bunk.

'Don't mind me, fellers. I'm not exactly house-trained either. Now where's that stew? The smell's churning me up!'

They all grinned. Ikey dashed out to his cook-house and staggered back with a black iron cauldron which he carried with the aid of a piece of sacking. It was steaming and brimful of stewed beef and thick gravy.

Gus looked at it and wondered how many days it would last. Not many, if his guess was right. They would be having it for breakfast as well as dinner and the gravy would be sopped up with some of Ikey's excellent biscuits.

It was when he was drinking his second cup of coffee that Gus brought up the subject of women. He looked around at them all, one youth, a middle-aged man and an old-timer. What kind of life did they have?

'What about women around here? I guess there's very few to choose from.' He sipped coffee while he watched the men look at each other. Ha ha, he thought, I've hit a nerve!

Jack spoke reluctantly.

'There's a half-breed widow-woman . . .' he began, slowly, then grinned when Gus didn't show disapproval but looked surprised. 'Well, it's like this,' Jack went on. 'A few years ago, Kit saved the life of this woman. A bunch of Indians were stoning her to death as a witch and because she'd took up with a white man. It happened near Pinetree Ridge where we have a line cabin. He watched what was happening from the ridge itself and as he told it, he was so angry at what they were doing, he let rip with his rifle and wounded the leader. The whole bunch scarpered, leaving the woman unconscious on the ground.'

'And then?'

'Well, he took her to the line cabin and cleaned her up of blood and mud and told her to stay there until she was fit. She stayed, too scared to leave. But it was a good thing for us. Ikey busted his leg a couple of months afterwards and she nursed him, going out into the forest and picking herbs and such to heal him with. There was some stuff called knitbone—'

Ikey broke in impatiently. 'He don't want to know about all that crap. He wants to know about us and her!'

Jack looked crestfallen. 'I just wanted him to know all about her, that's all. You won't turn her out of the cabin, will you, Gus?'

'No, why should I? She sounds very useful.'

'She is! Oh, yes, she's good for us! When we're out rounding up stray stock we make for the line cabin and we take her some grub . . . you don't mind her having some grub?'

'Not in the least.'

'Well then, she's grateful and . . . er . . . she makes it up to us. You know what I mean, Gus?'

'Yeah, I know. Very sensible of her.' Gus took another gulp of coffee to hide his grin. 'I might go and visit her myself one of these days!'

'You do that, boss,' Skip said eagerly. 'She'll be sure glad to see you!'

Ikey glared at him and slapped him on the cheek.

'You keep out of this, dumbhead! How'd d'you know what she likes?'

Skip looked sulky. 'She always welcomes me with open arms. . . .'

Jack haw-hawed and slapped his thigh.

'That woman's taught him all he knows!' He sighed. 'How I wish I had my time over again!'

Suddenly the amusement went out of Gus's eyes and they became cold and remote again. Time over again, eh? The thought unsettled him. It brought back the shock and bitterness of his mother's disclosure and her death. She'd been a good mother as mothers go and she'd provided him with a good father, but blood was thicker than water. He had to face his real father and find out what kind of man he really was. He only knew that he was ruthless with an obsession to own everything around him. He wanted to know the real man so that he could plan a revenge worthy of him. . . .

He got up abruptly from the table.

'Jack, if you've finished gossiping, let's have a

look at the horses, shall we?' Jack, seeing the look in Gus's eyes, got up silently and followed him outside.

Old Ikey stroked his bristly chin.

'There goes a complicated man, Skip. Don't ever get on the wrong side of him. I reckon the man's a born killer! I can smell death all around him!'

Skip laughed.

'Stop your kidding, Ikey. I know you and your tales. The guy seems OK by me. Mind you, he was a bit queer when I first met up with him. Made me feel uncomfortable and said I should call him, Mr Strang. A bit puffed up about himself. You reckon he's a bit loco?'

'Yeah, maybe I do. Who can tell?' Ikey started to clear away the dirty dishes. 'You can carry the stewpot back to the cookhouse and mind how you go. Then you can take the pig swill and feed the sow with the litter. She needs extra grub as she's feeding eight, and while you're doing that, catch the runt and kill it and I'll cook it up special seeing as we've got a boss at last!'

Gus and Jack went to the corral and looked over the mares with foals. They looked in healthy condition and Gus watched as they all pricked their ears and came galloping up to the barbed-wire fence to inspect them.

'Well . . . you know how it is, Gus. A feller gets fond of certain horses, and those mares are special. Kit bred them and he knew good horses when he saw them. He always said breeding counted and you got a lot more from breaking them in gentle-like than breaking their spirit. Many a good animal has been turned into a rogue because of bad management.'

'Yes, very true, Jack, but remember you can go too far the other way.' Then a thought struck Gus. 'Were there some of our horses amongst that stampeding bunch that Miss Marshall had gathered together for sale?'

Jack shook his head. 'No, God be thanked! We didn't reckon to have any right to sell anything without the owner's say-so. So this year we figured to wait and see what was to happen.'

'Very right and proper, Jack.'

'But we've missed out for this year, Gus. The army agents have come and gone. They'll be in Wyoming now and the ranchers there will be laughing all the way to the bank!'

'Don't worry about it. We'll survive, ' Gus said easily. 'Maybe we'll watch the youngsters and pick out a few extra mares to breed with and break in more geldings for next year. We might find other markets too. They're wanting horses back East, I understand. I'll check it out. Meanwhile, you can mark out a new corral, as I've some stock coming up from Texas. They're special. Appaloosas. And all pedigree stock. It will be interesting to see how they settle here in Montana.'

The rest of the day was spent in riding the range and rounding up the wild stock. Gus was pleasantly surprised with the quality and breeding.

'Kit Childs certainly had an eye for good stock,' he said appreciatively, and Jack went on to point out some of the blood-lines.

Gus and Jack found that they got on well with each other and Gus went to bed that night tired but happy.

The days flew by. Eventually Gus felt fairly confident about riding over his own land alone. Jack and Skip got on with their usual chores and Gus rode his boundaries.

Jack had given him a map of his holdings. Gus knew that the northern boundary was next to the Big M land, so one morning he reckoned to ride the southern border and make a few notes about pasture and water. He had been up since early dawn and was equipped with a war bag which carried his essentials, and his saddle-bags, full of his usual camping-out gear in case he should be caught a long way from home at dusk.

He was busy making notes in a tattered notebook when a single bullet whined past his right ear. A second later he felt the sting, as if a hornet had stung him. Dimly he was conscious of Susie rearing, her head coming back and cracking him on the skull. Then he was falling into oblivion and never felt the ground come up to hit him.

Gradually he came up out of the black void. He'd been in that void a few times in the past and recognized that he'd been knocked out. He groaned and then became conscious of cold water running down the side of his head. He put a hand up to his aching temple and came in contact with a hand. Opening his eyes wide, he looked up into the face of a woman. She was squatting over him and bathing his head with his own bandanna. Her dark eyes were anxious, but now she looked relieved.

'So you've come back to us,' she said in a thick sing-song patois. She smiled. 'You're lucky to be alive. Another inch and the bullet would have shattered your head.'

He tried to sit up but failed to do it. He felt as if all his strength had drained out of him.

'What happened?'

'Someone took a pot shot at you, and then bolted.'

'Why did he bolt?'

'Because I shot at him. I heard him scream so I

must have hit him. Here, have a shot of this. It's tiswin, made from corn.'

Gus looked at the earthenware bottle and sniffed its contents. He took a gulp. It fired his guts and he felt his energy return.

'Now that's what I call a real drink!'

She smiled. 'It's an old Apache recipe and I make it myself.'

'You're the medicine-woman who lives in the line cabin.' It wasn't a question, it was a statement.

'Yes, and you'll be the new boss. I hope I can stay here.'

He managed a grin. 'Now how could I turn a lady from her home after she came to my aid? I wouldn't dream of it!'

'Then you don't mind your men visiting me?'

'Of course not. It's your business entirely who you have to visit you. Might I ask where the line cabin is?'

'Just an hour's ride that away.' She pointed with her finger towards the foothills of a mountain range.

'What were you doing out here?'

She pointed to her horse, which was grazing at a distance. On the pommel were two jack-rabbits.

'I was out hunting game when I spotted a rider who was acting suspiciously. I could tell he was tailing someone and so I kept out of sight but followed close behind. I was beginning to think he was looking for the line cabin and me for I recognized him as one of Jed Wildsmith's men. But when I saw you coming over the pasture and stopping to write in your little book, I knew you were the one being hunted. But I didn't reckon on him taking a chance at such a distance and the shot was fired before I could do anything about it. But I hit him. I know I did and he rode off as if the devil was after him.'

'You saved my life. If you hadn't shot him, he would no doubt have come to finish me off. He probably thought my men were nearby. Thank you.'

He looked at her with admiration. She must have been forty or more, well-rounded with long dark hair, not blue-black like an Indian's, but parted in the middle, Indian-style, and braided in two thick plaits. She wore a Stetson, which was now hanging down her back. Her face was long, rather than rounded like an Indian's and her nose must have taken after her father's. She was olive-skinned and there were fine lines around her eyes. She looked as if she had suffered.

She wore old deerskin pants and a colourful printed cotton shirt, bought from some Indian trading store, and on her feet were handmade moccasins which covered her pants and came up to her knees. She was a fine-looking woman and it was little wonder that Jack and Skip and even old Ikey made the trip to see her.

Gus got shakily to his feet. He could feel the stickiness of blood running down his ear. He'd had a few bullet wounds in his time but never one in the head. She was right. He was lucky to be alive.

'Before I go, will you tell me your name?'

'My mother's people called me Yerba Twobloods. My husband just called me Yerba.' Suddenly she looked sad. 'He was a good man but my people killed him.'

'Yerba. It's a pretty name. What does it mean?'

'Yerba means 'good herb'. As my mother taught me what to look for in the forest I became known as the herb woman and so the people called me Yerba.'

'Well, Yerba, thank you for what you did for me. We'll meet again soon, but I think I have business with one of Jed Wildsmith's bloodhounds and it won't wait!'

Yerba looked at him in the eyes and he saw that now she was afraid.

'You're a hunter of men, aren't you? You've done this before but this time you might have met your match! There's evil waiting for you at the Wildsmith ranch! Don't go there! If you do, you will hear something you don't want to hear! I'm warning you. Keep away from that cursed place!'

He looked at her, standing straight and tall and proud.

'You really believe all that? You think a curse would come upon me?' He laughed. 'Nobody puts a curse on me. I'm the master of my own fate!'

'Even masters of their own fate can't fight against destiny! I'm warning you, boss of the KC ranch. You have done many things in your life-time that you are ashamed of and you have shut those things out of your mind. The poison is still there, deep down in your conscience. You will let it all out if you go to the JW ranch and the outcome will be catastrophic!'

Suddenly Gus was angry. The woman's words were already bringing back bad memories. He turned away from her and drew on all his strength to climb aboard his mare. He was dizzy and it was hard to focus, yet anger spurred him on. He would find that son of a bitch and kill him. He turned to Yerba for the last time.

'Hold your tongue, woman! There's nothing in what you say that will stop me from seeking out the man who tried to kill me! All I want from you is his name!'

They stared at each other for a long moment and Yerba saw that he was beyond reason. There was an aura of blackness around him that frightened her. She knew that she couldn't avert what was to be his destiny. She closed her eyes and spoke through clenched teeth.

'His name is Red Bartlet. You will recognize him because he's got hair the colour of the Flame God.'

'Thank you.'

She bowed her head in answer and he turned to ride away. He did not hear her whispered, 'May the gods go with you!'

FIVE

Jed Wildsmith was in the throes of a murderous anger. The bullwhip in his hand curled and whistled as it cracked down on the recumbent man's body. Great gashes of blood showed through the victim's torn shirt and he curled and twisted on the ground at each stroke of the metal-tipped whip.

A young girl was clinging to Jed's right arm in a fierce attempt to stop the whipping. She was screaming and crying and showed several facial bruises where Jed had hit her as he'd tried to shake her off, but she hung on like a vixen fighting her prey. But he was too strong for her; at last he loosened her hold on him and she fell to the ground. Then he turned his full attention again on the youth who was vainly trying to crawl away.

The whip came down twice more before a shot startled Jed and the men who were watching, wide-eyed, as young Luke Springer got the beating of his life. The men knew why he was being thrashed. Everyone knew that he'd been sparking Jed's adopted daughter, Jenny, a girl of seventeen. Jed had given all the men plenty of warning of what would happen to the man who tried to seduce his Jenny.

Now all eyes turned to the man riding leisurely into the ranch yard where all this was happening. Everyone was agog and wanted to see who had the nerve to go against Jed.

Meanwhile, sobbing, Jenny had crawled over to young Luke and was now trying to revive him.

Jed stood, the forty-foot whiplash curled at his feet, as he stared at the man walking his horse slowly towards him. But what impressed him most was the Peacemaker aimed at his belly.

'Let them go!'

'Who the hell are you to tell me what to do on my own property?' blustered Jed Wildsmith, mindful of the gaping barrel aimed at him which made the nerves up his back crawl.

'I'm the new owner of the KC ranch and I'm looking for a man called Red. Where is he?'

Jed Wildsmith's first reaction was to refuse to answer, but on second thoughts, after looking into a pair of murderous eyes which sent an icy whisper of something familiar through him, he glanced to his right and saw the men nearest Red Bartlet hurriedly moving away from him so that he was standing alone.

Gus followed his gaze and saw the big red-haired man standing with legs splayed and in the act of drawing his gun.

The Peacemaker no longer covered Wildsmith's belly, it was spouting bullets. Three shots were fired. One hit Bartlet in the gunhand and as the weapon catapulted from his grasp, a second shot hit him in the shoulder. Then, as he staggered forward a couple of steps, the third shot took him in the throat and he slumped to the ground.

Quick as a flash, Gus turned the gun on Wildsmith. Looking around he shouted:

'The first feller who reaches for his gun gets it and so does your boss!'

There was a dead silence. No one stirred and they could all see the boss sweating. Globules rolled down his cheeks and yet they were chalk-white. Gone was the bully. They saw him for what he was, a man who gave the orders for others to do his dirty work and face the danger.

One man spat in the dust and turned away. The others saw it and did the same until the yard was empty of men and only the girl and the youth on the ground remained.

Gus gestured with his gun.

'Help the girl and the boy!'

'*No*! I caught the bastard with my girl! He knew the risk and he'll have to go! As for her . . . I'll deal with her later!'

Now Gus faced a dilemma. It was to be a showdown but he could now see that the time wasn't right. He knew what dealing with the girl meant. She would probably come in for a beating.

He made his mind up fast. He'd killed Red. At least that chore had been achieved. Dealing with his father would come later.

He swung down from his mare and Wildsmith took two steps backwards, thinking that this cold-eyed stranger was going to do him physical harm. He put up his hands as if to protect himself.

'Leave me alone! Just get out of here!'

'Don't worry. I'm not after your hide now,' Gus answered contemptuously, 'I'm taking these two with me.'

'No! Take the boy but leave the girl!'

Gus ignored him. He scooped the girl up in his arms and tossed her lightly on to Susie's back. He was contemplating how to manage the youth when there was a commotion and a bunch of riders swung into the yard. They stopped with a flourish behind them.

Gus turned and saw that Kate Marshall and Yerba headed the group with Jack Jones. All looked concerned. Jack edged forward. 'You OK, boss?'

'Yep.' He glanced past Jack to Yerba. 'I got him. He's one less for you to worry about, Yerba.' Then he touched his hat to Kate. 'Howdy, ma'am. We look as if we're gathered together for a hoedown!'

But Kate ignored his attempt at jocularity. She and Yerba were attending to Luke Springer and the girl Jenny. Kate only answered with a snappy, 'You should have had more sense than to come alone!' and went on helping Jenny to clean up a cut on her arm.

Only when Yerba had finished cleaning up the blood from Luke's back did she have time to look at Gus. It had been five days since he had galloped off and left her and his appearance shocked her. He had lost weight, his face was gaunt, and that part of her which was Indian sensed that during those days and nights ghosts from the past had stalked him.

It was all there in his eyes. She wondered what kind of hell he'd been through sometime in the far distant past, which now had been brought back to life. Why had it all surfaced now?

Gus felt he was in an unreal world, thrown back to the time when he'd been known as Jeb Stuart's right-hand man. Jeb Stuart had been General Robert E. Lee's top spy until he had been shot at the battle of Yellow Tavern in Virginia, and from then on, Gus Strang had taken his place. The job hadn't only entailed spying on the Federals, but also seeking out those traitors to the Confederacy, officers who deserted with their men in the midst of battle, men who were paid to sell the secret strategy plans of coming battles. So many skirmishes were lost because of betrayal and General Robert E. Lee exacted revenge when officers he trusted failed to carry out their orders.

Major Gus Strang was the instrument of that revenge.

He was the general's bloodhound and showed no favour. He gunned down brother officers if they were traitors. He showed no mercy to those who had once been his friends.

The time came when killing was just a chore. He hardened his inner self and shot a man in the back if it was possible for he had come to hate looking a man in the eyes as he was shot down. He gave no quarter and asked for none himself. The only satisfaction he got was to report back to the general that the job was done.

Now, he felt again the soul-destroying blackness creeping over him. It had come down as soon as he aimed at Red Bartlet and pulled the trigger of the Peacemaker, and it had not left him.

He gave the man he knew now to be his father

one last look before he eased his horse into a canter. Yerba was right. This place was evil, or was it because the man he was to track down was his own flesh and blood?

He kicked Susie fiercely in the ribs. Squealing in protest she set off at a mad gallop. Instead of making for the gate out of the yard, he set Susie's head for the wire fence. Susie took it, soaring high into the air and over. Both she and Gus needed to vent their feelings.

Behind him, Jack Jones and Skip and some of Kate's men backed off warily, guns out for fear any of Jed Wildsmith's men felt they had to do something.

But no one offered to stop them.

Yerba had Luke up behind her, his head on her shoulder, an arm clinging about her waist. Jenny was up with Kate, her horse following behind Yerba's.

It was then that Jed Wildsmith broke out from a kind of stupor.

Jenny . . . don't go, Jenny!' But Jenny did not turn to look at him. 'Jenny . . . for God's sake, Jenny, don't leave me! You're all I've got!' The cry was despairing but the horse walked on.

Then Wildsmith grew angry, his face reddened.

'Jenny, you come back at once! Do you hear? Goddammit! I took you in from that wagon train when you could barely walk! You owe everything to me! Is this the way you repay me?' Jenny never turned her head to look back. 'Jenny, I'm warning you . . . if you go with that young fool, you're no longer my daughter! You hear me?' His voice ended in a scream.

He watched her and Kate reach the yard gate. Then suddenly, as if in a frenzy, he reached for the gun at his side. As his men around him gasped, he aimed at Jenny's back. His foreman managed to lunge forward and knock his arm upwards. The bullet sailed harmlessly over the women's heads.

At once there was an uproar. Several guns were fired and Jack Jones cursed. He didn't want a confrontation, for they were outnumbered if it came to a gun battle. The time wasn't right for that and in any case it was the old man who had started the shooting. Nothing to do with his men.

'Right, boys.' His stentorian voice rang out. 'Let's ride and to hell with those bastards!' The bunch of men put spurs to their horses and rode out on to the trail that would lead them first to Kate Marshall's land.

Behind them they could hear Jed Wildsmith screaming but no posse followed them. They rode on through the night, only stopping to eat and rest the horses and to give Yerba a chance to change Luke's bandages and to give him a drink from her bottle of tiswin, which put some life into him for a while.

Jack kept a look-out for Gus but that first night he did not join them. He was far too busy fighting his ghosts of the past. Only when the sun was going down on the second day was he seen riding across country to join them.

Jack Jones watched him come with narrowed eyes. He said to Kate who was riding beside him:

'There comes a man bedevilled. God help him, because he's a good man at heart.'

Kate did not answer. She only watched him come and join them.

Kate reckoned Jenny and Luke should stay with her and Yerba would come by when she could to bring herbs and watch for signs of fever. The days passed and Luke gradually improved. When he recovered some of his strength he helped around the ranch by chopping wood and carrying water.

Jenny looked happier and the frightened apprehensive look began to disappear. Kate heard her laugh occasionally with Luke and was pleased for her. Jenny was also a welcome female companion for Kate who hadn't realized the lack of a woman's company before.

Gus, in the days that followed, tried to put his father out of his mind to ease the black depression hanging over him. But that feeling of preparing for a hunt still haunted him. He knew someday he would have to face his father and settle it one way or another. But one didn't shoot a father in the back. It would have to be face on, looking into his eyes, giving him a chance. Not that he was afraid of dying. He'd faced death often enough in the past. But death to him was a coward's way out. A bullet in the right place and then *poof!* nothing. At least a bullet would put an end to this black cloud surrounding him.

He hid his depression from Jack and Skip and only Ikey guessed that he was still troubled. But when his herd of appaloosas finally arrived, he cheered up at the sight of the pedigree herd. They were a beautiful sight in their differing colours of bay with the darker markings which denoted the breed. Gus knew they were the product of Nez Percé mustangs bred with Spanish horses going back to the time of the Conquistadores. His father, Ned, had often told him the story of the Spaniards who'd come to conquer the new land of America and it had been Ned's passion for appaloosas that had fired Gus to go on breeding them. They were a famed breed for both riding and farm work. Ned Strang's horses were famous everywhere in Texas.

Now Gus was curious to see how they adapted to the lush Montana pastures.

They were turned into the new corral, all one hundred of them, the best picked out from his herd in Texas on his father's old ranch by his trusty foreman. He knew Hal would only send the best they had. Now, after a few days to get over the journey by trail and by rail, they were settling in. Soon, Gus would cut out the best mares and a couple of stallions and keep them corralled, the rest would be freed to roam the range with Kit Childs's stock and perhaps they would get some good crossbred foals in the future.

Gus spent his days amongst the mustangs, examining and assesssing, and he felt his black mood lift. Running practised hands along muscled backs and down rumps and fetlocks, he gradually absorbed the feeling of getting back to nature.

He came back to the ranch one day at noon, tired and ready for some of Ikey's excellent stew. He had been up since dawn, mending the corral fence where some enterprising stallion had jumped it and broken down a couple of fence posts.

He washed up, ducking his head in the horse-trough in the yard and shaking the drops from hair and shaggy beard. It was good to feel the brackish water slaking away the sweat.

Then, as he turned to go into the cookhouse, he heard the drumming of hoofs. What the hell? He turned. Shading his eyes from the glare of the sun, he saw a small bunch of riders coming lickety-split down the trail towards the ranch.

They were getting close when he recognized Kate, with Jenny and Luke and some of Kate's men. He stood waiting for them, concern growing as he saw their condition. They'd been riding for hours and their horses' heads hung low as if the animals were giving the last of their strength.

When they finally rode into the yard, Jack and Skip were with him. Ikey stood at the door of the cookhouse with a ladle in his hand.

Gus ran forward and caught Kate as she almost fell from her horse. She was dirty and sweaty and she smelled of woodsmoke.

'What the hell's happened?'

Kate lifted a heavy head, nearly too exhausted to speak. 'They came for Jenny and they set the barn on fire and the wind sent the flames towards the house.' She sobbed. 'Everything's gone, Gus . . . gone up in flames! But we got away . . . The smoke . . . it hid us . . . the men . . . some of them are dead. They tried to stop those bastards . . . They kept calling for Jenny, but we were lucky. We'd all been out riding, rounding up strays, so we got away.' She collapsed in Gus's arms and he carried her into the house, while Skip helped Jenny and Jack show Luke and the three men with them into the bunkhouse, where they could clean up and rest.

Then Ikey brought in plates of stew for all and with it some baked yams and fresh biscuits and some of the corn beer that he made. Gus was full of smouldering anger as he ate. To Kate, he seemed cold and remote. She never dreamed of the conflict going on inside him. But by the end of the meal he knew what he had to do.

He must face his father and take the revenge he'd planned so many months ago.

Later, when Kate was more rested and willing to talk, he asked her for more details of the raid.

'They seemed to come from nowhere. We were riding in with some of our horses when suddenly we saw smoke coming from the buildings. The barn went up, flames shot high into the air . . .'

'They fired your hay, one of the tricks we used during the war.'

Kate barely heard Gus as she pictured the scene and its horror in her mind. 'The wind blew the flames to the blacksmith's shop and then the corner of the ranch house caught fire. I'm worried about Lew and Jacko and Carlos. We heard shots and Carlos galloped off to help Jacko and Lew. He disappeared into the smoke. Then we heard shouting and someone was yelling for Jenny to come out of the house.'

'Then what happened?'

'We heard more shots and Luke dragged at my bridle and shouted that we should get away as far as possible while we could. He knew and I knew that if we were captured, Luke and I would be crowbait and Jenny would be taken back to become Wildsmith's prisoner again.'

'Prisoner?'

'Yes. She told me that he was very jealous. He didn't want her talking to the men, or riding by herself. He kept telling her that she owed her very life to him and that she was his daughter and must obey him in everything. He wanted her sole attention and she couldn't stand it any longer. If it hadn't been for Luke, she says, she would have killed herself long ago.'

Kate saw Gus's eyes grow remote. She shivered. What was going through this strange man's mind to make him react this way when talking of Jed Wildsmith?

Gus left her abruptly and sought out Jack Jones who was checking his guns in the bunkhouse.

'I want to talk to you, Jack.'

Jack laid down the rifle he was putting together after cleaning.

'Yes, Gus. I guess it's about Wildsmith?'

'Too right. This situation can't go on. The old

bastard has patience and he has everyone on the range on tenterhooks wondering when and where he's going to strike next. The Marshall place could be just the first burn-out. It could become a habit if no one goes against him.'

'But what can we do, boss? He's got at least twenty men to call on and half of them are professional killers. The small ranchers can't afford to run a big crew. Kate's been singled out because she's taken Luke and Jenny under her wing. He'll send men here next!'

'I'm going to see him, Jack!' Gus spoke firmly and with finality of purpose.

'You mean alone?' gasped Jack. 'It would be madness? You wouldn't have a chance!'

Gus smiled.

'I'm not going to ride in with all guns cocked on me. Oh no, I'll do like we did during the war when we were hunting. . . .' He stopped and Jack saw that puzzling look he'd glimpsed before which put the shivers up his spine. He swallowed.

'Do you want me to come with you?'

'No, you'd be a liability. I couldn't watch your back while I'm watching my own. What I want of you, Jack is to run this ranch with Skip and Ikey if I don't come back.' He pulled a stiff parchment out of his pocket and opened it up. 'This is the deed to the ranch and I'm deeding it to you and the others in the event of my death.' He took a stubby pencil out of his pocket and wrote the necessary words. Then he signed it. He offered the pencil to Jack. 'Can you write? Sign your name here, as witness to what I've written.'

'But I can't write!'

'Very well. I'll sign for you and you put a cross where I say.'

Jack was very quiet when it was all over.

'I still don't like you going on your own.'

'Forget about me, Jack, and think of the others. You'll be responsible for the women and Luke. You'll have to be vigilant for the next few days so organize things well. Think of it as a siege.' He clapped Jack on the shoulder. 'You can do it, feller!'

He turned at the bunkhouse door.

'By the way, don't tell the others what I'm up to. There's no need for the women to worry. Tell 'em I'm on a round-up of the horses. Tell 'em I'm more concerned about my appaloosas than I am about what's happened to them!'

'But that makes you out to be . . .'

'A bastard? But that's what I am, a bastard.' He grinned.

Gus packed what he needed and took a look around him at what had been his for such a short time. A great place to live and raise a family, he mused. He didn't reckon on his chances of coming back to raise that family. He knew only too well the risks he was taking. He would have to reach Wildsmith fast before he was rumbled.

After that, events could look after themselves.

He felt cold and unemotional, just as he'd schooled himself many times before when he'd gone on the hunt. But this time was different. Would he be able to shoot his father down cold-bloodedly? Or would his hand waver at the last minute?

He shrugged the thought aside. Thoughts like those could be his undoing.

He whistled for Susie in the paddock where she spent her days when they were not together out riding. He saddled up after inspecting her legs and shoes. At least the old girl was raring to go.

Then, with no one watching him go, he cantered away and was soon out of sight of the ranch.

Jed Wildsmith slapped his foreman's face and failed to see the sudden flare in the man's eyes. The blow was hard and the man staggered back, one hand to his flaming cheek.

'I told you, boss, she wasn't there! She and Luke and the Marshall woman must have been out on the range.'

'Then you should have spread out, all of you!

Didn't it enter your thick head that if they weren't around the buildings they would be on the range? God dammit! Must I do everything around here? What the hell do you think I pay you good money for, if not to think for yourself? Jesus H. Christ! I'm surrounded by fools!'

The man listening bent his head. The slap had set off a loose tooth, the result of a bar fight, to aching. Shooting pains ricocheted through his skull.

'Will you shut up?' he screamed suddenly at Wildsmith. 'I'm sick to death of your rantings! You foul-mouthed, yellow-streaked son of a bitch! You can't do the job yourself because you've got no balls and you think you can steamroller your bullyboy ways on me? You might frighten those jerks,' he nodded at the small crowd of men who had drawn close because of all the shouting and who were watching what was going on with interest, 'but I've had enough. I'm quitting and you can go to hell'

'You go to hell on my say-so,' ground out Wildsmith. Then he looked around at the watching men. 'Any more think like he does?'

No one stirred or blinked an eye. There was tension in the air and one wrong move could signal disaster.

The foreman looked wildly round at the men.

'Come on, fellers, back me up! You know what we said in the bunkhouse!'

There was a scraping of feet as the men moved uncomfortably but no one looked the foreman in the eye.

'So what was said in the bunkhouse?' asked Wildsmith softly.

The foreman stared him fiercely in the face.

'Like I said, we don't like your bullyboy ways, especially when that daughter of yours is involved! We're not paid to hunt down a young girl!'

'You've never objected to other jobs I've ordered you to do!'

'Harassing folks and stampeding cattle is one thing but going after a young girl and beating Luke just because he sparks her, is way beyond what I'm ready to do!'

'So are you saying you deliberately let them get away?'

'No, I told you how it was, the fellers can bear me out.'

'And you won't ride out and hunt them up?'

'No!'

Wildsmith's soft voice should have warned him.

'Very well. From this moment onwards, you no longer work for me!' As the foreman turned away he suddenly called sharply, 'Bono!'

The man swivelled to face him.

'Yes?' He stared into the barrel of Wildsmith's gun. As his eyes widened there was a sudden flash and Bono wasn't aware of his aching tooth any more.

Wildsmith stood with the smoking pistol in his hand and gestured to one of the men who were watching, aghast.

'Take him away and bury him!' He limped back into the house.

He flung himself down in the old leather chair and reached for the bottle standing on a small sidetable. He uncorked it with his teeth and drank deeply, enjoying the fire in his guts. That was the only way to treat rebel underlings, he told himself. Bono was trash anyway. He took another drink and then sombrely wondered whom amongst the men he could trust to take Bono's place.

They were all trash! Every goddamn man in the world was trash! And all women were trash! Even Jenny, the little blue-eyed toddler whom he'd taken in from that wagon train when her folks were killed. Goddammit, even she was trash! Jenny, the one person he loved in the world, the untouched daughter he'd spoiled and pampered and been so proud of. Now she was despoiled by that young upstart. She was like all the rest, trash . . . trash . . . trash!

Two tears came trickling down his cheeks. He wiped them away as if they shamed him, and took another drink in a bid to forget but he could only see Jenny in his mind's eye, growing up, laughing when she sat on her first pony, her fat legs hardly able to span its belly, the way she kissed his cheek when he brought her a gift from town and the way she sang about the house when the snows were gone and the first days of spring arrived.

He was going to miss her dreadfully. Damn her! Damn . . . damn . . . damn her!

He emptied the bottle and threw it with a crash into the stone fireplace, The shards of glass spread all over the hearth.

The small Chinese cook looked round the door at his master, but saw he had passed out, his head back against the leather of the chair, his mouth open and snores reverberating around the room. Quietly, the cook shut the door and crept away. It was time to pray to his dragon gods to bring peace and harmony back again.

Gus rode on during the night hours. He could move swiftly on his own and cut across country to save time. Time. He had to be there before the men were up and doing their chores. He wanted to surprise Jed Wildsmith in his bed. He was looking forward to seeing the shock on the old man's face when he woke him with a nudge from his Peacemaker.

At last, just after the false dawn, Gus paused on the ridge looking down into the valley where Jed Wildsmith's ranch and buildings lay. The spread had all the hallmarks of a prosperous ranch, white picket-fences, barns and outbuildings neatly arranged around the main house. He saw that the bunkhouse was well away from the big sprawling ranch house. No doubt Jed Wildsmith liked his privacy away from his men.

He took his time to study the lay-out, using his field glasses and ranging slowly over the terrain. A small corral holding several mares and foals was adjacent to a stable and barn which would cater for the comfort of the mares. He nodded to himself, satisfied that his plan would succeed. He would fire that barn. It was well away from the bunkhouse and the panicking squeals of frightened horses would alert the men.

The trick would be to set the blaze so that it didn't take hold too soon and for him to race to the ranch house before the crew scrambled from the bunkhouse to fight the blaze.

He wondered how many men were standing guard. It seemed that Wildsmith was too confident to have many men on the night shift. He spotted the flare of a match and guessed there was a lone man watching the mares and foals. He wouldn't be expecting an attack from the small ranchers, but would be watching out for a prairie wolf who might find the courage to go after a newly dropped foal to feed her young.

He ground-hitched the mare, who was trained to stand with bridle reins hanging loose in front of her, so that she could come at a whistle. Or, perhaps in this case, grow tired of waiting if something happened to him, so that she would make her way back to her stable. He ran lightly down the steep incline and keeping in shadow of the pine rees, he managed to come alongside the corral fence. Then, carefully, he moved forward, his feet touching the ground lightly as he'd been trained to do in the army, and inched his way towards where he calculated the guard to be.

Now he sniffed tobacco smoke. He stopped until he had located the exact place where the man would be lounging. Taking his well-used army knife he snaked forward, slowly and deliberately and eventually came up behind the unwary guard. For a long moment, Gus watched him contemptuously. If he'd been a member of his troop he would have had the son of a bitch shot for sloppiness.

Gus took a long deep breath and pounced, his arm going about the man's neck, his bulging muscles cutting off the man's air. The knife in the other hand jabbed at his neck under his ear.

'Try to make a move and you're dead!' he hissed as the man vainly tried to free his throat. At his words, the man collapsed and lay still, his eyes peering wildly to get a glimpse of whoever was holding him in the deathlike clinch. Then Gus watched the eyes close as he became unconscious. Swiftly, Gus roped his hands together and then fastened them to the man's ankles, leaving him trussed, his back bent like a bow. Gus was gasping with exertion. He estimated the man would be out for a couple of hours, if he was lucky. To make sure he couldn't sound an alarm, he tore the man's bandanna from around his neck and made it into a gag. He was now well and truly hogtied.

Running along the fence, he found it easy to get lnto the barn. It held hay and straw and pitchforks, sacks of grain, several sets of harness and a huge jar of linseed oil. Everything that a pampered mare or foal might need.

Gus ran his eyes over the floor space. Yes, he'd found the right spot to start a fire. He moved quickly, for the light was getting stronger now and soon the first cock would crow. He had to get a move on.

The fire was small to start with and he left a trail of straw which led to the main bales of hay.

It would take some time for the fire to creep along the ground. Gus was satisfied. He'd used this trick before.

Outside, he ran lightly to the back side of the ranch house and found the rear door into the yard unlocked. Inside, he listened. All was quiet. It was too soon for Wildsmith's houseboy to be up and doing. The cook would be in his cookhouse, but Gus reckoned it was still too early for him to be astir.

Silently he crossed the wooden boards to what he reckoned to be a bedroom and opened the door quietly. He looked in and saw the big double bed, spread with a faded patchwork quilt. He heard the bedsprings creak and knew he'd found Wildsmith at last.

He tiptoed across the room and gazed down at the old man, who was snoring gently. He watched him with mixed feelings. He could so easily have killed him where he lay, but the bastard would never have known anything about it.

Gus wanted him to know fear. Wanted him to know who he was. That the man about to kill him was the fruit of his own loins.

He sat down on the edge of the bed and felt Wildsmith's legs move under the covers. He drew the Peacemaker and cocked it. The sound must have disturbed Wildsmith's sleep, or else some instinct in him smelt danger. He opened his eyes and looked up at Gus. Gus savoured the look of shock on his face.

'What in hell are you doing here?'

Gus had to give him full marks for not showing the fear he'd expected. The feller had nerve, like his own, he thought wryly. He leaned forward, staring into eyes so like his own ... slate-grey, cold eyes now flickering with fear as they stared back at him.

'I'm here to talk about a girl called Rosita. You remember her?'

Jed Wildsmith licked dry lips. Yes, he remembered the full-bosomed Rosita with a mixture of feelings.

He nodded faintly.

'What about her?' Then, wondering what in hell this man knew about Rosita, he struggled up on to his elbows. Gus's gun reminded him of the need for caution.

'Rosita Gonzalez was my mother.'

'So? We all had to have a mother!'

'Have you forgotten? Is it so long ago you've forgotten you threw her out when she told you she was pregnant?'

Jed Wildsmith stared at him for a long moment and then threw his head back, laughing.

'You think I'm your father? That hot-assed

bitch was a slut! She bedded every goddamn feller in my crew! Your father could have been anyone of a dozen randy bastards!'

Gus felt the rage engulf him as he heard the words pour fron Wildsmith's mouth.

'You're lying! My mother wasn't like that! You dirty foul-mouthed slimeball! I should kill you now for what you say about her!' He lunged forward grabbing the old man by the throat. 'The thing is that a shot would be too good for you!'

'Hold it, feller! You weren't around to know what she was like!' Wildsmith's fingers clawed at Gus's fist holding him. Gus relaxed his hold and the man he thought of as father lay back on the pillow, gasping, his chest rising and heaving as he tried to draw breath. 'If you want to know the truth, ask Chuck Gilroy, the oldest man on the spread. He'll tell you what kind of girl she was! God knows he slept with her often enough when I was away from the ranch!'

'You're lying again!'

Wildsmith shook his head wearily.

'I wish to God I was. I thought Rosita was my woman. But all the time she was enjoying my men at my expense. They were all laughing at me behind my back. They thought it was a great joke, bedding the boss's woman. Then I came home unexpectedly from a cattle drive and found her in the bunkhouse all cosied up with the cook. That was when I threw her out!' Then he raised his head tiredly and looked Gus full in the face. 'Do you think I'd throw her out if I thought the child she was carrying was mine?'

Gus was now feeling sick. It couldn't possibly be true about his mother. She had never looked at another man. Ned Strang had been the only man for her.

But he stared into Jed Wildsmith's eyes, eyes so like his own.

'I still say you're my father. Perhaps you didn't treat her right. She told me on her deathbed that you were my father. Why should she lie when she knew she was dying?'

Jed Wildsmith closed his eyes, a tear glistened at the corners.

'I loved her, you know. That was what made me so bitter. I wanted a child. That is why I took Jenny in, and she's turned out to be trash!'

'Because you were so jealous and wanted to own her body and soul. Was that what it was like with my mother? Was that why she acted the way she did? And when you threw her out she had her final revenge on you? Is that why she told me so that at last she had her final revenge?'

Jed Wildsmith's eyes roamed all over him.Could it be possible Rosita had been telling the truth? He shook his head in pain and pushed the thought away. Then rousing himself, he said harshly,

'If you're going to shoot me, get it over with or get out!'

Gus drew a sharp breath and held the Peacemaker firmly pointing to Wildsmith's head. His finger was slowly pressing down on the trigger and Wildsmith's lips tightened. The bastard was going to kill him!

Then the bedroom door burst open and one of his men was standing there.

'Boss! The whole damn spread's going up in flames!'

Gus's hand jerked and the bullet tore into the ceiling rafters.

SIX

Gus swivelled. His second shot, aimed at the newcomer, went wild. The quick reaction from a professional gunslinger took Gus in the fleshy part of his shoulder. His head was slammed against the iron bedpost, knocking him out. As he slumped across the foot of the bed, the gunman drew a bead on him to finish him off but Jed Wildsmith shouted at him.

'No! I want him alive! You go back to the fire!'

'But the fire's heading this way! The wind's freshening up. You've got to get out of here and you can't drag that son of a bitch outside yourself!'

'Then help me get him out!' Wildsmith scrambled out of bed and in just his grey woollen vest and long johns, took Gus's legs while the gunman took his shoulders. They heaved him outside just as the cookhouse beside the main house burst into flames.

'I'll see to him,' gasped Wildsmith. 'You go and help fill the water buckets!' With perspiration rolling from him and choking on the smoke from the fires, Wildsmith tied Gus up to a heavy wagon wheel lying propped up against a corral post.

Then he limped away to oversee what they might save. To his horror, he saw that all the buildings were fast turning into blackened shells. A great anger shook him. He had a good mind to go back and shoot the bastard. After all, the man who claimed to be his son had been going to shoot him!

He turned away, sick at heart. All the long years of bulldozing his way to wealth were now wasted. He was too old to start again. He wanted to make Gus Strang suffer.

Cursing, he limped back to where he'd left Gus unconscious and tied up securely. He was still out cold, lying just as Wildsmith had left him. Now, he studied the face and body of Rosita's son. Was he this man's father? Forty years of hatred and a secret grief because of Rosita's betrayal of him, were hard to forget. Had he been wrong all those years?

Gus's eyes opened and they stared at each other. Cold slate-grey eyes locked on to cold slate-grey eyes and it was Jed Wildsmith's eyes which finally turned away.

Sick beyond anything he'd ever experienced before, he now knew. All those agonizing years when another man had brought up the boy who should have been his!

Gus's lips twisted.

'Well, old man, have you come back to shoot me?'

Kate Marshall expected to see Gus at breakfast but he hadn't shown up, old Ikey told her. She'd raised her eyes a little at this, but went about the business of helping around the house, seeing to Luke's healing injuries and washing out her underwear. But when noon came and still no Gus, she buttonholed Jack who'd been mending fences with young Skip, at least that was his excuse for watching the trail. They were all aware that they might get visitors from the JW spread looking for Jenny.

Jack seemed to be avoiding her and Kate was a bit peeved. It had taken some time to find him and pin him down.

'Where's Gus? Why isn't he here? He must know that we might get visitors!'

Jack coughed and looked sheepish.

'He's kind of concerned about his appaloosas.

He wanted to find out how they were settling in with our mustangs. The stallions can be ornery bastards, especially if some of the mares come into heat. Stallions can do a lot of damage to each other.'

'Yes, yes. You're not telling me something I don't know! What I want to know is why he's got to go now, just when all hands are needed here! Surely he knows what might happen!'

'I'm sorry, ma'am. He thinks a lot about his appaloosas. I think he loves horses more than people!'

Kate's eyes flashed.

'Well! If that's the way he thinks, I'm sorry for him!' She flounced away and Jack shook his head. He hadn't been very tactful, but he was a plain man and didn't go in for fancy talk.

The afternoon dragged on and Kate was in a foul temper. No matter how she tried to resist the urge, she kept looking to the far horizon to see if she could see Gus riding home.

Then, after snapping at Jenny and Luke for something trivial, she made her mind up to ride out and take a look around. Maybe she would come across the herd of horses and Gus and if she did, she would give him a piece of her mind. Yes, by God, she'd ask him outright whether she and Jenny and Luke were an embarrassment to him.

If so, they would depart and go to one of the other neighbours.

She returned just before dusk. She'd come across several small herds of horses but no Gus. Now she was really worried. Had he been set upon by Wildsmith's men and thrown into some deep crevasse?

She found Jack feeding the mares and foals in the corral. She saw that he'd seen her and ducked away. So the son of a bitch knew something he wasn't telling her! She might have known it from his earlier sheepish manner.

'Jack!' It was a peremptory cry. 'I want to talk to you!'

He shambled across the yard, head down and when at last he looked at her his eyes were shifty.

'Jack?'

'Yes, ma'am?'

'You know what I want to talk to you about. Where's Gus?'

'Like I told you, out somewhere on the range . . . looking over his horses.'

'You're lying, Jack. Now cut the crap and tell me what's up!'

Jack gave a big sigh. He took off his hat and rubbed his brow while he tried to think fast. Goddammit! This female was razor-sharp. Why didn't she act like other females and concentrate on the kitchen and vegetable-plot? He knew the answer to that, of course. Kate Marshall had always acted more like a man than a woman. She needed a good strong man to tame her. Gus Strang could do the job. . . . He grinned.

'What you think you're laughing at?'

Jack swiped the grin from his face. She was uppity enough without knowing why he laughed.

'Look, ma'am, he told me to say nothing. It's up to him what he wants to do, so take my advice and believe what I'm telling you. He didn't want to worry you womenfolk.'

He knew that was the wrong thing to say as soon as he said it. She pounced on the words.

'What about this worrying the womenfolk? Now out with it, Jack or else I'll shoot you where it hurts!' Shocked, he saw her drag her Colt from its holster. It was firmly targeting his groin.

'You can't mean that! By God, you're a devil witch,' he gasped, as he noted her determined expression.

'I don't make threats I can't carry out,' she replied, menacingly. Inwardly she was shaking. God knows what she would do if he challenged her to make her threat good, but she comforted herself that no man would gamble with his tackle at risk.

'Holy Mother! Be careful with that thing! I don't want to end up a gelding at my time of life!'

'Then talk, Jack, and stop fussing. If Gus has done some fool thing like going over to the Wildsmith spread, I want to know! I'm no city miss who'll faint when she hears a swear word. If Gus is in danger, we should all do something about it!'

So Jack told her what Gus had done and she was appalled.

'I don't know what he had in mind, but he was stark raving mad when he knew you'd been burned out. He was in a hell of a rage when he rode away. I must say, I'm mighty worried myself that he hasn't come back.' He hesitated for a moment and then went on: 'He made me sign a paper . . . for fear he didn't come back—'

'A paper?' she broke in. 'Let me see it!' He brought forth the stiff crackly paper from where he'd kept it in his vest pocket. 'I meant to give him it back when he returned,' he said lamely.

Kate read the paper and saw that it was the deed to the ranch, and the scrawled words making Jack and Skip and Ikey the owners if he did not live.

She stared at Jack with shock, then returned the paper to him.

'Jack, we've got to do something about this. Gus doesn't expect to live. Hell's bells, Jack, you should have come to me earlier!'

'He didn't want you to know!'

'You fool! As if it mattered what he wanted! It's his life, dammit! We've got to go over there and do something! Jack, round up Skip and my men and be ready to ride.' She ran across the yard shouting for Jenny.

Jenny appeared at the door looking both frightened and curious.

'What is it, Kate? Is Father coming?'

'No, it's Gus. He's gone to see your father. I want you to saddle up and ride to Jesse Lowe's place and tell them what's happened. Get Jesse to send a man to all the other ranchers. We've got to stop your father once and for all. Now get into some riding-pants and get going!'

Well, old man have you come back to shoot me? The words reverberated in Jed Wildsmith's brain. He looked down at Gus; blood oozed from the shoulder wound, but Gus didn't betray the pain he must be suffering. There was a smile on the hard lips, a mocking kind of smile which Wildsmith was tempted to wipe away with a clenched fist.

'You son of a bitch, and she *was* a bitch, I assure you,' he said between clenched teeth. 'Killing's too good for you! You sure hit me where it hurts! Why didn't you come in and just tell me who you were?

But to fire the whole goddamn place . . . you know how long it's taken me to get to where I am today? And now all gone because of you!'

'All built on climbing on other folks' backs! Preying on the weak and taking advantage and being ruthless!'

'Who are you to talk about being ruthless? I can see it in your eyes! You're a killer too!'

'Then you admit I'm your son!'

'No! I admit nothing. It just means that we are two of a kind! What you want you get, just like I do. Out here, a man either grows strong and takes, or he's beat and he goes under. You're a survivor just like me but that doesn't make me your father!'

'You're a stubborn old bastard! What about Rosita? How did you treat her? In the same way you've treated Jenny?'

'Jenny? She turned out to be trash!' Gus heard the pain behind the words.

'Because you made her so. She's a good girl, Wildsmith, and Luke's a good boy. You should have been proud that she chose wisely.'

'Nonsense! He's just a drifter, a rolling tumbleweed! He's got nothing but his horse and saddle. She didn't need anyone but me! She would have had everything after I'm gone,' Wildsmith went on bitterly, 'but she threw it all away!' He looked around him at the smouldering, blackened remains of the buildings already ravaged by the fire which had now passed on. 'Now, there's only the land and the stock, and it's all your doing!' His gun came up and was levelled at Gus's head. 'You deserve to die!'

Gus closed his eyes. This was it. He'd faced death many times. Death was no stranger . . . He waited for the final explosion.

None came, but instead he heard a gasping choking sound. He opened his eyes cautiously and saw Jed Wildsmith crumpling to the ground held by a grinning Chief Elkhorn.

'Elkhorn! How did you get here?' Gus gasped. Then reaction set in and he felt the pain of his arm swoosh up into his head. He fainted.

When he came round, he found himself loosened from his agonizing position, with Yerba kneeling beside him and cleaning up his wound. He grunted with sudden pain.

'Careful,' he grated, 'that hurt!'

'No wonder,' she said caustically. 'I've had to remove a scab of blood. You're lucky. The bullet went through the fleshy part of your arm, so quit whingeing and lie still while I fasten this bandage.'

'How come you and Elkhorn are here?'

'I was up early tending to a calf and I smelled

smoke. I watched as the sun came up and I saw the black smoke in the distance. I was curious to see what was happening. I hoped it was Wildsmith being burned out. It was and I've never been so happy in my life!'

'And Elkhorn?'

'He saw the smoke too and was coming to investigate. He and his braves were watching at a distance. Then we met up with your man, Jack Jones. He had the woman, Kate Marshall, with him and a bunch of riders from the ranches. Can't you hear them? There's a gun battle going on back there!'

Gus struggled to sit up. Yerba was right. Now that he could concentrate, he could hear muffled shots coming from around the main house.

'Then I'd better go and help them.' He tried to rise. She pushed him back.

'You lie still. You're in no fit state to start a war. You'll set that wound off bleeding again if you do.'

'It's my left arm. I can still shoot with my right fist!'

'You're not indestructible,' she said brusquely. 'I think there's someone back there who'd be most upset if you cashed in your spurs!' They gazed at each other and Yerba's lips lifted in a tight smile. 'Believe me, Mr Strang, it's time to come to terms with your past life and put it behind you. You are at the beginning of a new life. Don't waste your chance!' She turned to melt back into the undergrowth.

He gazed after her, suddenly oblivious to what was going on all around him. She turned and gestured to him. 'Come, don't wait to be shot like some felled steer! Up, man, and make yourself invisible!'

Light-headedly he scrambled to his feet. He was weaker than he'd thought possible, so, gritting his teeth he made for the undergrowth.

Jenny watched Jesse Lowe's men ride away towards the place she'd known as home ever since she could remember. Jesse had sent his cook's boy to the next ranch with the news of the Marshall outfit being burned out. Now they were all heading to the JW ranch to get Wildsmith and sort him and his men out for the last time. It was to be war.

Jenny cried. She was all mixed up. She hated her father for what he'd become these last years and for what he'd done to Luke. She remembered the time when she was small and she'd loved him. She had been his pet and nothing had been too good for her. When had it all changed?

Was it when she had come to womanhood? She couldn't rightly remember. The change had been slow and subtle. Was it when the men started whistling at her and passing jokey remarks about her blossoming into an attractive female?

Whenever it was, it had become insufferable. She couldn't even smile at a man or make a light-hearted reply to a joke. He watched her at all times, would only let her ride out on the range when he was with her. She had become a prisoner of his unreasonable jealousy. If it hadn't been for Luke she would have either killed herself or run away, risking danger in the wilderness from animals or Indians, rather than live that life any longer.

But now she thought of her father as he used to be and cried. She felt like a Judas, and she couldn't stand it. She must ride out to the only home she'd known and perhaps seek him out and ask for forgiveness.

She'd been told by Jesse Lowe to stay at his place but she couldn't do that. She must know what was going on.

She made her mind up and with tears still wet on her face, rode out to her adoptive father's ranch.

She passed within a few miles of what was left of Kate Marshall's ranch and buildings and averted her eyes. Smoke still rose lazily in the air and the smell invaded her nostrils. It was a reminder of what her father was capable of. But she carried on, regardless.

She heard the rattle of gunshots well before coming in sight of the spread. What she did see shocked her so much she wanted to vomit. The blackened shells of buildings she knew well. Only the house, which stood at quite a distance from the rest, was still standing. Smoke rose in wisps all around and she could see that there was a siege going on. Gun flashes came from windows and to her amazement she spotted Indians as well as white men hiding behind boulders and scrub, surrounding the house at a distance.

She saw Jesse Lowe and his men spread out and join those who were already holed up and the exchange of gunshots was savage.

Then as she watched, she saw a half-naked Indian run like a deer towards the house, a burning brand in his hand. He threw it and it landed on the shingled roof before rolling down on to the ground. The brave turned away with a triumphant whoop, but the triumph had come too soon. Jenny saw him throw up his hands before hitting the ground. He raised his head but it flopped back to earth and he lay still.

The burning brand lay smouldering. It wouldn't be long before there would be another try.

This time it wasn't a man who threw the brand, it was a burning arrow that did the trick. Jenny gasped as she saw the arrow thud into the wooden shingles, and quiver a little. Then a slow lazy smoke began to rise from it. Soon, the wind would gently waft the smoking ember into flame and then those inside would either die or come out to be shot!

She drew a sharp breath. Her father must be in there with his men! Oh, God! What had she done?

It was all because of her and Luke. She should never have contrived to see him! She never dreamed it would come to this.

She spurred her horse to a gallop. She didn't know what she could do to stop this carnage but she had to do something. Even if it meant riding into the yard and becoming a target for the men both inside and outside the house.

Jenny cut across country by an old favourite trail and came towards the house from the rear. There was an old line cabin close by. She would tether her horse there and go the rest of the way on foot.

It was then she found her father, bound and gagged and stretched from a beam in the hut, his toes barely reaching the ground. His head hung down on his chest and he had been beaten. A pile of dry wood was around his feet and she could see that one burning brand would set the whole cabin ablaze in a flash.

'Father!'

The head lifted and the eyes opened.

'Jenny? Is it really you, or am I dreaming?'

Quickly Jenny looked around for something to cut her father down. She found an old knife used by the cowhands when cutting up a steer. She slashed at his wrist bonds but couldn't save him from slumping to the ground when the last strand was cut.

He lay on the pile of wood, gasping.

'Who did this?' Jenny asked huskily as she struggled to help him off the wood pile. He rubbed his wrists and looked at her with a mixture of love and loathing.

'Chief Elkhorn. Evidently Gus Strang is an Indian-lover,' he said viciously. 'God damn him to hell!'

He stood upright and stretched.

'What will you do now?' she asked fearfully. 'They've set fire to the house!'

He groaned and shook his head.

'So that's it! A lifetime's work gone up in smoke!' Then he turned on her and his eyes were those of a maniac. 'It's all your fault, you dirty little slut!' Before she knew what was in his mind, he slapped her hard across her face.

She fell to the ground, half stunned. He limped away into the smoke and she heard him untie her horse and ride away.

She lay where she was and silent tears trickled into the dry earth.

She knew that that would be the last time she saw him.

Jed Wildsmith was past reasoning. Anger and bitterness raged through him. He'd lost Jenny and the thought of Gus Strang brought back memories he'd tried to forget. Now, through the man who claimed to be his son, his spread, which he had been so proud of, was gone and it looked as if the ranch house itself would go up in flames if he didn't do something about it.

He would seek out that ghost from his past, and exorcise it once and for all. He hadn't much else to lose. If he survived, he would be back where he started, with the land and some stock. He couldn't face starting all over again at his time of life.

If he was to die, he would take that bastard with him.

The horse charged through the undergrowth, panic-stricken because the strange man on his back was using him cruelly and because of the noise of the firing ahead.

Suddenly Wildsmith saw movement. He checked the horse's wild gallop. Someone was out there in a small clearing. He edged the animal closer and the figure squatting over what looked like a bundle of bloody rags rose to face him. It was Kate Marshall and she had a bloody bandage in her hand.

She recognized Wildsmith and drew herself up, with chin in the air. She spoke in a firm voice even though inside she was quaking.

'What do you want?'

He leaned forward and smiled broadly as he pulled out the Colt from its holster.

'You!' Carefully he got off the horse, keeping the gun pointing at her.

'What do you want with me?' The wild look of the man frightened her further. She knew his nerves were stretched to breaking point for she saw the tic at the side of his mouth as the muscle twitched. One wrong move and the trigger-finger could stiffen and fire. She couldn't take her eyes away from him. Her breath came in gasps.

'We're going to take a walk . . .' he began.

'No! Skip's hurt bad! I can't leave him,' she said helplessly, hoping for some compassion from him. None came.

'I say we'll take a walk! I don't care a shit for your man. You're going to stop this bloodshed.' Before she knew his intention, he had a hold of her wrist and was twisting her arm behind her back. She was now in front of him. 'Walk!'

Together they walked through the undergrowth, the horse following behind, until they came to the ranch yard. He waved his gun hand in the air.

'Stop the shooting! Or I'll kill the girl!'

The men holed up in the house ceased firing and stared at the boss walking out into the line of fire. Jack Jones cursed where he was hidden with his men along with the neighbours' men who were scattered around the building.

Chief Elkhorn raised his hand and gave two long whistles. All became still.

'What is it?' Gus asked Yerba as she strained to see why everything had gone quiet. Gus was propped up against a tree. He still felt light-headed but his strength was returning.

'It's Wildsmith,' gasped Yerba, 'and he's got Kate and he's holding a gun on her!'

Gus struggled to his feet, cursing softly.

'I'll have to go and face him. It's me he wants!'

'No! You can't go! You're not fit!' Yerba was horrified. Gus was still leaking blood.

Gus gave her a tired smile.

'I'm fit enough for what has to be done. After all, I'm his son. We both know it, but he won't face up to it!'

Yerba's eyes widened in disbelief.

'His son? So *that* was the trouble I saw as a black aura around you! I can't stop you. You are

153

meeting your destiny at last!' She watched him walk slowly towards the clearing in front of the house.

Chief Elkhorn watched him emerge into the clearing and he held his hand up to his men. It was plain to see that the white man was ready to challenge the old man who was holding the girl prisoner. Gus walked forward and then stood wide-legged fifty paces from Wildsmith and Kate.

'Let her go, Wildsmith. It's me you want!'

Wildsmith laughed crazily. He looked back at the ranch house where the fire was quietly taking hold. It hadn't got to the stage of bursting into flame but everyone watching reckoned it would be only another hour and then it would be too late.

'What I want is gone. I don't even care any more that the house will burn. It's done. Finished.'

'What about me?'

'You? As a man I want you dead! You ride into my life and create disaster. Everything has gone wrong because of you!' Wildsmith turned to the house, waving. 'What in hell are you waiting for? If you want to live, then get out there and put that fire out! Organize a bucket brigade! Must I think of everything myself?' Then he turned again to Gus. 'You took Jenny in and that bastard, Luke. I'll never forgive you for that!'

Gus shrugged.

'You blame everyone but yourself, old man. Let Kate go and we can talk this out. You want to kill me? Then let's do it fair and square!'

'You don't fool me, Gus Strang. If I let her go I've lost my ace. I know how your mind works, because it's like my own. You're a devious bastard . . .'

'Like you. I also keep my promises. If I say I'll kill you, I will!'

Wildsmith laughed.

'You want to kill me but you can't because I'm your father! I want to kill you but you're my son and I can't!'

'So you admit that I *am* your son?'

'You say you are. I don't see any resemblance to me, but your eyes give you away. You've got the same ruthless non-forgiving quality inside that head of yours! You're a killer like me!'

Gus shivered. He knew, but no one had ever told him to his face before what he was. Yerba had sensed it. Was it there for the world to see? If it was, then he should die here and now.

He raised the Peacemaker and pointed it at his father, who promptly hitched a wilting Kate in front of him.

'It's a stalemate, Gus Strang!' Wildsmith called.

'Get those men of yours away from here and that redskin pal of yours. Get them off my land and then we'll really talk!'

Gus looked behind him and saw that Jack Jones and the rest of the ranchers and their men were there, drawing closer, watching and waiting.

'All right, boys, back off, and Chief Elkhorn, if you're listening, it's all over. It's between me and Wildsmith now.'

But there was no response from Chief Elkhorn.

Gus took a quick look around.

'Chief?' But there was no sign of him and the braves who had been with him were no longer there. They had all melted into the undergrowth.

Kate struggled a little, her eyes pleading as she watched Gus. The Colt pressed into her neck.

'Keep still, you bitch, if you want to keep your head!' Wildsmith snarled. 'Well?' he called to Gus, 'what are you waiting for? Tell those bastards to go home. I've got a ranch house to save and those goddam men of mine need a kick up the ass to get them moving!'

'Not before you let Kate go!' The time's come when you can't issue orders, Wildsmith. You're finished! You're no longer king of the range. It's *you* who's got to ride out! You'll never make a home here again! The ranchers won't let you! Get it?'

'This is my land!' screamed Wildsmith. 'No one can take it away from me! And I'll say who comes and goes, so get out, all of you! Go on, give the order, Strang, or I'll shoot the woman!'

'Shoot her and you're a dead man, I promise you.' Gus's voice had taken on an ugly note now, and the trigger's being cocked could be heard in the deathly silence.

'You wouldn't dare!' shouted Wildsmith.

'Try me! Go on, shoot her . . . and find out!'

Suddenly there was a commotion. Screams and shouts filled the air and everyone's eyes turned to the gate of the yard. There was Jenny, struggling with Luke who was trying to hold her back. She was fighting like a wildcat to get away from him.

'Father!' she screamed, and both Gus's and Wildsmith's focus was turned on her as she broke away from Luke and started running towards them.

Then it seemed that everything happened at the same time. Wildsmith's hold on Kate relaxed and she fought to free herself. The old man's gun arm came up and caught her on the side of the head. Gus, seeing Kate fall, swivelled sharply, raising his gun and aiming at his father, but Jenny got in the way of the shot and the bullet blasted its way into the shingled roof behind.

Gus started to run towards Kate, who had slumped to the ground, when there came a shot from the back of the house. Gus watched his father straighten up, a look of surprise on his face and then he pitched forward to lie face down. Gus looked to where the shot had come from and saw a grinning Chief Elkhorn crouched behind a water-butt. He nodded to Gus and then stood upright. Raising his arms to the sky he gave the Apache victory howl. Then, as Gus watched, he disappeared into the undergrowth and was gone.

Gus knelt down beside his father and gently turned him over. There was a peaceful look on his face, all lines smoothed away. He was still alive and breathing shallowly. His eyes roved over Gus and his lips stretched into a rictus smile. He coughed a little and there was the oozing of blood from punctured lungs.

'Shot in the back,' he coughed. 'I never thought. . . .' A gout of blood streamed down his chest, which heaved as he gasped his life away.

Then he lay still for a while. After a time, his eyes opened again. They had lost their cold arrogant look. They were the eyes of a tired old man.

'We'll never know, will we?'

'Know what, Father?'

The lips smiled at the word.

'I wish I'd heard you say that long ago, boy. But it's too late now.'

'What can't we know, Father?'

'Would either of us have had the guts to kill the other? We'll never know now!' He gave a great sigh and then his eyes closed for ever. Gus looked down on him and could feel no emotion whatever.

He knew the answer to the question. If the old man had shot Kate he would indeed have shot his father.

He turned weary eyes on the crouching woman who was sobbing silently and gently picked her up. She looked up at him and he smiled.

'It's all over, Kate. It's time to start all over again. Come, I'll take you home.'

'I haven't got a home, remember? It's all burned out!'

'You've got a home with me, sweetheart. We'll start afresh and help Jenny and Luke to make over the JW ranch and then we can all live in peace with our neighbours. That's what you want, isn't it, Kate?'

She looked up at him, eyes suddenly shining and the plain homely face was suddenly beautiful for him. She nodded still looking at him.

'Yes Gus, that's the thing I want most in the

world!' He bent his head and kissed the wide generous mouth and at that moment he felt reborn, felt the secret coldness around his heart melt away. The past was dead and gone. This was a whole new world he had entered into.

Gus felt he had at last really come home.